FREE TO BLOOM

FREE TO BLOOM

JILL GREEN

ADVOCATE HOUSE
Sarasota, Florida

AUTHOR'S NOTE

This is a work of fiction. The real people, places and events have been molded by memory, changed by time, and altered by necessity, like confetti thrown into the air to settle into a totally new pattern.

Copyright © 2011 by Jill Green
All rights reserved.

No part of this book may be reproduced or transmitted in any form, by any means electronic or mechanical, including photocopying, recording, or any information storage and retrieval system now known or to be invented without permission in writing from the author, except by a reviewer who wishes to quote passages in connection with a review written in a magazine, newspaper, or broadcast.

For information regarding permissions, write to:

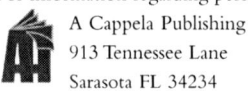
A Cappela Publishing
913 Tennessee Lane
Sarasota FL 34234

Designed by Carol Tornatore

Manufactured in the United States of America

Library of Congress Cataloging-in-Publication Data:
Green, Jill.
    Free to Bloom / by Jill Green. —1st Advocate House paperbound edition.
    p. cm.
1. Fiction. 2. Romance. 3. Adventure—Costa Rica.

ISBN 978-0-9846177-2-2

Acknowledgments

I want to thank my friend, editor and publisher Pat Vaughn for her constant encouragement, inspiration and education. She and our writing group, especially Marisa Magnani and Marita Hermann, taught me how important critiquing and editing are in the creative writing process. We've all become good friends as we supported each other through the birth, growth and maturity of our books and stories.

I am wholly indebted to my network of wonderful friends family and sweetheart Bob who have made my life rich and this book possible.

For my brave and adventurous son Ray and daughter Nicole

"And the day came when the risk to remain tight in a bud was more painful than the risk it took to blossom."

Anaïs Nin

CONTENTS

Of Time and the Mountain	1
San Anselmo	9
Getting to Know You Costa Rica	17
Fear of Falling	23
My Friend George	29
The Last Resort	35
God's Caveman: PART ONE	49
God's Caveman: PART TWO	57
Getting to Know You–Humbolt County, CA	61
Puppy Love	67
Alligator Dreams	49
Fault Lines	85

Of Time and the Mountain

My daughter Guiselle and I finish our shopping at the central outdoor market in San Isidro and head for the Chirripo Hotel to pick up my husband. Will travels back and forth to Costa Rica, keeping his job in the States but spending a month in the summer cutting through the bureaucratic red tape involved in our new adventure—buying property and building a house in a foreign country.

I look at my watch, "Come on Guiselle, we'd better hurry. You know how your father hates to wait."

"How could I forget, Mom?" A worried look crosses her face. "And check out those clouds. They're gathering awfully early today."

The pace of our lives is going to accelerate while Will is here. I sigh. Of course I love that the family will be together, but the sparks always fly. The three of us are such strong individuals, and stubborn to boot. I've taken a leave of absence from teaching so Guiselle and I can handle all the details of getting the house built on the southern Pacific coast while Will keeps the money coming in at home to pay for everything. Before construction can begin, the road has to be graded and rocked, local workers hired, and supplies ordered.

Guiselle is the key to the whole process. She's the only family member fluent in Spanish. It puts a big burden on her because she has to handle all the ordering, complaints, mistakes and misunderstandings. Though just out of college, she's proving quite capable. Her years of living alone in foreign countries, especially Argentina, have given her a strong advantage. Though her independent nature makes it easier to deal with problems, her lack of business acumen gives her a sharper edge than necessary when dealing with the laid back culture of Costa Rica. In that respect, she's like her dad.

I try to keep things on an even keel and handle the more menial tasks that always need to be done. I'm the sounding board for both Will and Guiselle. Trying to hold the stress levels down becomes my major focus as I try to instill in them a bit of the 'patience is virtue' attitude of the local people.

It doesn't really work, but they're right about one thing: the rainy season will soon be bringing daily torrents of rain. The road will become a sucking, sliding hazard and the wood won't dry enough to use. We have important deadlines to meet if we want to finish the house by the end of the year. The money won't last forever. I know I'll have to go back to work soon. Wish I didn't. Living in the little old farmhouse close to the river makes me very happy. Life is so much simpler here, filled with the important tasks of living a primitive existence in the tropics. Not boring.

I look up from my reverie to see Will already sitting on the patio of the Chirripo sipping *café con leche*. A tall thin man, reflecting a sense of urgency in the forward thrust of his tight shoulders, he moves quickly through life. When the everyday snags delay the completion of his goals, his irritation surfaces, his fair-skinned face reddening easily from sun, embarrassment, exhilaration and anger. So many things on his mind, surfacing willy-nilly like bubbles in a boiling kettle. No one knows what to expect.

"Hi Danielle, I've missed you." Smiling, thank God.

"*Hola,* Hon, it's so good to see you. I give him a quick hug and kiss.

"Hi Dad, what good timing!" She hugs his neck, sees him looking at the gathering clouds. "Just finished shopping and we're ready to go home." Guiselle knows what to say.

Will takes the wheel as we start out across the mountains to the coast on the two-hour trip back to the farm. The clear-as-cut-crystal afternoon is a complete contrast to the last five days of wet gray. The month of June brings with it the consistent rains that turn *verano* (summer dry season) into *invierno* (winter wet season). In Costa Rica the distinction in seasons depends on precipitation, not temperature.

The mountains rise above the strip of raw unpaved highway running the length of the Pacific coast. The sun shines a halo of light upon the peaks, illuminating the jungle in iridescent green, criss-crossed with gaily-strung ribbons of red clay roads winding in and out of view around the curves. The stark shocking beauty always surprises me as I follow the slope of the hill down to the clear aqua depths of the sea. A white foam line of breaking waves is interrupted by the coconut palms swaying in the ever-present offshore breezes. "It's just like in the movies, but we're in this one," I whisper.

As the ribbon of road straightens out for the last few kilometers before the drive up our mountain, I notice the looming clouds presaging the afternoon downpour. "We're just going to make it before the rain turns the road to mud." Guiselle can see Will's face reflecting those clouds as the old worry creeps in.

"Before we return to the farm house, I want to check the altitude of the house site with the altimeter watch I brought," Will says. "I need to test the water in relation to the altitude to guarantee that there's enough flow for the hydro-pump to work." Because of the steepness of the grade he locks in four-wheel drive for the last segment of the journey home. Guiselle and I have worked on this part of the road with Bolivar, the caretaker, filling in ruts with rocks and gravel to keep it passable between torrential downpours for the only car (ours) in the village. But during the *tormentas* even the horses have trouble not sliding.

The rain begins to fall as we start up the hill. Will leans over the steering wheel as Guiselle and I anticipate where the worst ruts and slides will be. The rain progresses from drops to buckets in a matter of seconds. The top layer of wet clay begins to slither under the tires as the backend of the car begins its sideways cha-cha-cha.

"As long as we keep our forward momentum going we'll be fine," Will barks as we slide too close to a steep drop-off.

"Dad, maybe we should just leave the car and walk the rest of the way," gasps Guiselle.

Will loves a challenge. "We'll be fine, I said." The rock-filled ruts hold us steady as we jerk along pure clay, rock boulders, and past the giant *ceibo* tree that marks the entrance to the farmhouse.

"What the hell are you doing?" I yell over the crashing rain. "Up here there's nothing but wet sucking clay."

'We're so close to the house site. Just thought I'd drive up the last few meters to get my altimeter reading." Will angers.

"Please, Dad, let's wait until the rain stops. This is the steepest part, without any rocks to grab onto."

Will is determined and now irritated. With no place to turn around anyway, he continues up until the tires are slick as silk sheets. No matter what he does with the brakes, clutch or gas, our forward momentum slows, stops and reverses the faster the wheels turn. The car gracefully slides backwards into the ditch on the side of the road and stops, balancing precariously on the edge of the cliff.

We burst out of the car, saving ourselves from certain death, as Will plans his next strategy.

"I knew it," I take a deep breath. "Leave it. Until it stops raining."

"No. I can get it out of here, goddamit!" He looks at the wheels and, trying a back-and-forth rocking motion, only spins the front tires in deeper and the back ones closer to the edge.

Guiselle's protestations of, "For God's sake, Dad. Stop!" make Will all the more determined to get the car out of the scrape it's in.

His temper rises with the color of his face. "Give me some fucking credit," he yells above the thundering rain. He jumps out and begins wildly tearing off wide flat banana fronds to cram under the wheels for traction.

"I can't stand to watch! I'm going to find Bolivar to help

us out of this mess." I retreat down the trail through the rain forest to the farmhouse.

Guiselle follows me, calling back to her father, "Why do you always have to be so stubborn? And controlling?" We leave him with the car teetering on the brink.

The separation is good, giving everyone time to calm down. "Why is it Will can't use logic when he gets into these crises?" I'm the calmer one, slower to react. Not the emergency lifesaver that Will is. Walking through the dripping jungle, my constricted chest begins to relax as I suck in hot humid air. I realize that my horrid stress and anxiety returns only with Will.

Leaving the United States and incorporating myself into a slower life and culture, time has become a different entity for me. And Will isn't around trying to change things. Guiselle and I are in charge of building our dream house in Costa Rica—a retirement retreat in a primitive tropical environment away from the development that ruined our Gulf coast hometown.

I'm beginning to understand the *manana* attitude of the Costa Rican *campesinos* (country folk). Time isn't something to beat, it's a continuum of life from morning to night. It makes sense. There's no high technology (or even low) to make things faster. Since it takes all day to saddle my horse and ride down to the village for supplies, I might as well enjoy the ride: the howler monkeys calling, a concert of parrots on stage in the *ceibo* tree, a friendly *'hola'* to a neighbor passing by. Gringos, on the other hand, hurry, hurry to finish everything fast, get the news first, make the most money. And for what? To get bored because there's nothing left to do? Workaholics.

On the isolated spot where Will and I have chosen to build there are no phones, no electricity or paved roads. What at first had seemed like a long walk down the mountain now has become just the common method of travel. The amount of time it takes doesn't matter. Day follows day in a succession of sameness. It's more important to blow a milkweed into the air and watch its delicate descent than to reach a destination *a punto*. Stress has slowly seeped out of me as acceptance has seeped in.

   I don't like that returning feeling of tension shooting adrenalin through my body, but Will loves it. It makes him feel alive. After twenty-five years of marriage, is this the emotion that'll separate us? We've had a good life, wonderful children and friends. Is this tension going to crack us apart like the constant tremors on this faultline in Central America? After just a few hours together it's all coming back.

   As the jungle opens to the old farmhouse I now call home, I declare aloud, "I can't live this way anymore. He'll be falling off this cliff one way or another for the rest of our lives. I don't need to be afraid with him anymore. I'm no longer afraid without him."

San Anselmo

Nestled between the coastal mountains of Costa Rica and the Pacific Ocean stands a small old farmhouse. Weathered boards and tin roof overlook a ridge where the rain clouds gather each afternoon before spilling over into the valley. Every summer life returns. Shutters open to air the house, bright sheets and towels flap in the breeze, and the trimmed garden all give the farm an air of comfortable occupancy.

Will and I have been vacationing in San Anselmo for several years. I sit alone on the front porch at the end of what might be my last summer here. I take a deep breath and release it, forcing myself to recall the events that led to this point.

My husband and I had been looking for a natural retreat for the summer months, away from the tensions of traffic, jobs and deadlines. We bought the farm and took on the difficult task of carving out a place for ourselves in the lush tropical mountains, trying not to upset the balance of nature and the local culture. We both loved the calm and beauty of this place and had been hoping that it would soothe our chaotic relationship.

This summer we'd started working on a new house overlooking the ocean. I remember climbing the hill to the construction site that first day to meet the local crew, carrying hot coffee and *arepas*, sweet pancakes, for the traditional afternoon snack and siesta. The sweat drips from my brow and dampens my shirt. The crew appreciates that I continue their customs in the hot tropical climate.

"*Café,*" I call out unpacking the steaming bottles of coffee and unknotting the crisp white cloth from the *arepas*. I watch the men descend the scaffolding: strong, short, muscular and as graceful as wild cats. We'd been lucky to hire all local men from our pueblo, San Anselmo, that is within walking distance of the house site. We are the only people on the mountain to own a car. The workers are in splendid shape from leading healthy simple lives on the edge of the rain forest. Their hardworking ways and willingness to learn makes up for their lack of technical experience.

Will introduces me to Juan, the crew chief. He smiles and says, "*un minuto,*" as he finishes pounding a nail at a precarious angle. I watch his small muscular body climb effortlessly down the ladder, his face lighting with friendliness. His dark, piercing eyes look admiringly at me, the tall, blond, blue-eyed gringa. "*Como esta?*"

"*Bien, bien.*" I smile.

"*Salud a los otros. Marvin, Jaime, Luis, y Ronald.*"

"*Hola, hombres. Como estan?*"

"Todo bien." They answer in unison.

Juan knows more English than the others and replies, "nice to meet you."

My daughter, Guiselle, has returned to college. I've taken over as interpreter for the construction and liaison between Will, who doesn't speak Spanish, and all the local people, whether workers, suppliers or neighbors. It isn't easy. There's much more to translating a language than knowing vocabulary.

"Quisiera trabajar contigos." I offer my skills.

Juan points to his hammer and asks, *"Sabe usted como usar un martillo?"*

I nod, "I've pounded many a nail."

He laughs, *"Que valiente!"*

I turn to Will to translate and notice that strange frozen smile on his fair, sunburned face as he glances from Juan and back to me. 'Oh shit, it's the jealousy thing again,' goes through my mind as my smile freezes a bit too. I choose to ignore the look, deal with it later, and explain to Will that the men think it strange that a woman would be working with them.

I pitch right in. They're surprised but eager to help me. *"Vamos a ensenarle el trabajo."* Juan offers to show me their methods. I glance at Will, but he has turned his big stiff back to them as he pointedly goes back to work. Every now and then I can feel Will's eyes on me, watching as I climb easily over the framing, brushing damp hair out of my face. Then he peers at the men to see if they're noticing me too. Especially Juan. Of course they are. He sees the men looking at me, a total contrast from their women who still adhere to a division of labor for the sexes in this undeveloped part of the countryside. The men appreciate my skills, but don't know how to handle me. Should they treat me as a woman or an equal? Can they do both? It will take a while for them to get used to a woman working along with them and even telling them what to do. Women on the campo don't work with men. Their sisters, daughters and wives have plenty to do at home, having babies, taking care of the homestead, keeping the floors polished to an eye-squinting sheen. They rarely leave the valley or even their own doorsteps. The men have all the freedom allowed by a huge double standard, typical in Latin America. It's okay to philander a bit as long as they love and honor their families and wives.

When work is done for the day, Will leaves quickly. I linger on to help tidy up, put away the tools and visit with the crew to get to know them and their culture better. Tired and apprehensive, I drag my feet down the hill toward the farmhouse knowing we'll be having one of two conversations: The Dr. Jekyll or the Mr. Hyde. Will greets me with a big smile, "Well, what did you think of the crew? Great guys, huh?"

Thank God for Dr Jekyll. "Yup. They're friendly and really hard workers."

"What about Juan? Think he'll make a good crew chief?

"Don't know yet, but the others seem to respect his knowledge. He's willing to learn our ways, but wants us to learn and accept his too." I start to relax.

"He's handsome don't you think?" forcing brightness. "I saw all those guys giving you the eye. They're not used to having a woman on board, especially a good-looking blond *gringa*."

Will's personality is changing in direct proportion to our foundering marriage. He goes from being proud of my independence to jealous and possessive. It's getting worse now that we're living apart for long periods of time. I have taken the summer off from teaching to supervise the house construction, because Will can't. He returns for a week now and then to 'check on things'. This project is supposed to be an antidote for our waning relationship. Instead it's taking a crazy turn. The longer we're apart the more erratic he becomes, the less I want to be around him.

As the summer passes I learn to wield a wicked machete and can pound a nail with the best of them. Juan tries to make things easier for me when tempers flare or mistakes are made from language misunderstandings. He's not afraid to say *no comprendo* instead of nodding 'yes' like the other men, whether they understand or not. Our friendship grows as our conversations expand from construction talk to events and people outside the close quarters of our small valley. I catch myself watching him as he works. He's so different from Will; small, light on his feet, flashing dark eyes.

Will and I were the first foreigners to settle into the community. The local people welcomed us. During the summer dry season fiestas are held once a month in each of the surrounding pueblos. The women and children only attend the ones in their own community, while the men and boys make the rounds to the outlying areas by horseback. This makes for a scarcity of females at the *tournos*. I attend as many as I can. It's my chance to socialize, meet some of the people around the valley, and counteract my loneliness from living alone most of the time.

This month's *tourno* is farther away, on the next mountain. Juan and his brothers drop by to catch a ride in the car making the trip much shorter. I ask if Nita, Juan's wife, and the other women want to come along.

"*No quieren ir.*" They don't want to. All *Ticos* (the diminutive for Costa Ricans) love to dance as much as I do, especially to those Latin rhythms: *salsa, meringue, cumbia.* The men are thrilled to find a new attractive foreigner who knows their dances and take turns asking me. But I usually end up with Juan. He's proud to have the *gringa* on his arm and I'm happy too. I love dancing with him as he holds me close, swinging me through the tight intricate moves.

"Are you liking this?" he smiles, looking straight into my eyes.

"*Que divertido!* What fun!" I flash.

"*Que romantico!*" he counters.

I feel alive. I love it. Will flashes into my mind. He's never liked to dance except when sloppy drunk. This is sick. I hate him. I hate myself for being too afraid to break away, for justifying my little private fantasy to get me through.

On his last visit before the end of the summer the growing friendship between Juan and me makes Will very edgy. "I was watching you work on the site today. Did you know that little cotton top you were wearing shows the outline of your nipples?"

"I don't think so, but…"

"And when you bend over you can see them even better. Are you doing this for me or for Juan?"

"I'm not doing it for anybody. It's hot here; I wear the coolest thing I can find. What are you getting at?"

"I've seen how you look at Juan, even though I don't know what the hell you all are laughing and talking about."

"Are you jealous? This whole scene used to be your fantasy. You loved to show me off to other men," I scoff.

"I still do. Come here." He yanks me to him, holding me tight, putting his face into the curve of my neck, lips to my ear. "Tell me how he makes you feel. How wet you get just thinking about him."

I freeze. Can't do this. But if I don't he'll get angry. Maybe violent. I'm scared. I close my eyes until I see rainbows and dream of making love to Juan.

Will leaves early to see the lawyer and file the land title in the capital. Breathing a sigh of relief I stay on to close up the house, set up the caretakers and say my good-byes. I've never been happier to see him leave.

After making all the arrangements, there's still time to descend one last time to my favorite paradise on the river. The grotto with its natural pools still stuns me with its beauty. Sunning nude on the rocks after a cool swim, a flash of color surprises me. No one usually disturbs me here. Juan appears through the trees. He knew where I'd be. Our eyes meet in silence asking no questions. "I've come to say good-bye." He breathes. Before I can react or speak his hug takes my breath away, our lips barely touch. I hesitate, "Will you swim with me?"

"Por supuesto." We slowly separate as I help him remove his clothes, savoring every new touch as my fantasy becomes real. The blue pool surrounded by gentle rainforest lures us. An ibis silently appears at the end of the tunnel the river makes through the jungle, disappearing around the curve. Through the constant rush of water over the falls we hear the myriad voices of birds unseen in the canopy. Butterflies

drift above our heads, touching down before darting away again.

Juan and I slip into the cool water, a delicious contrast to the heat of the sun. Then we emerge like frolicking otters shaking rainbows from our glistening bodies. We hold hands laughing and slipping on wet rocks, until we reach a dry smooth plateau in the shade of the giant ceibo tree. Our sliding hands and whispering tongues meet no resistance on wet skin. His fingers drift under my arms feeling for the slight lift of my breasts, slowly moving over the roundness, seeking the peak of my nipples. My head falls back with a quick intake of breath as our necks intertwine, his lips on the taut skin of my throat. His hands shiver across my body, dip into my waist, circle the dark shadow of my navel, following the line of hair below into the small triangle curling around his fingertips into a breaking wave.

But the crash of a rock tumbling into the river breaks the spell. I turn to see someone retreating through the jungle. My hot blood turns to ice. Will. How long has he been there? "My God, Juan! It's Will." I'm shaking. "What's he doing here? Something must have happened to the car. A landslide?"

"Tranquilo! Tranquilo!" He tries to calm me down. *"Que vamos a hacer?* What are we going to do?"

Before he can stop me I grab my clothes, race up the hill and round the curve to the house. Will's not waiting in the yard. No matter what happens I must confront it. I fling open the door. Silence. "Will? Will?" Nothing. I remember the gun in his room, in the drawer by his bed. He keeps it around for killing poisonous snakes. Gone. But who's the viper here? Me? Juan? Will? I go out on the porch to sit, staring at the sun as it pierces the rolling front of clouds, and wait.

Getting to Know You—Costa Rica

The first spark of attraction crossed between Adrian and me on a dusty mountain road in Central America.

"God damn it!" I squat in the Costa Rican dirt. My tire's flat.

Shielding my eyes from the sun's glare I don't see Adrian until he leans down. "Got a problem? Maybe I can help."

"Oh, hey Adrian. You bet." My smile cracks wide open at the sight of him. His vivid gray eyes spark from a handsome face encircled in tight peppery curls. Dimples on either side of his upturned mouth set off the quote of a brushy moustache. We'd met at a party the previous winter and, when I'd found out he knew about alternative energy systems, he was nice enough to answer my numerous questions.

After helping me change my tire he ratchets the last of the lug nuts tight. The sweaty job complete, our eyes connect for just a moment longer than necessary. "You're good to go, Danielle." He claps his hands free of dust.

"Muchas gracias. You're a lifesaver."

"Glad to help. I like a woman who's not afraid to get her nails dirty."

"I'm learning. Living here alone breeds dirty nails."

"What happened to your husband? Haven't seen him around much lately."

"He can't leave his job in the States except for a week now and then. I'm handling the house construction. It's easier when Will's not here. Anyway I really appreciate the advice you gave me on solar and water systems. There's so much to learn. I've never lived off the grid before."

"Just a city girl?"

"Yea, but I hate the thought of going back to it next week. I love it here."

"Me, too. How long will you be gone?"

I shrug. "I'm going to see if my marriage can be salvaged, but it doesn't look good."

"Well, if it's a rusted hulk," Adrian chuckles, "get in touch when you return. I'll be back after New Year's."

* * *

Home in Florida, my husband and I sit at an outdoor café and become personal. We're not supposed to do that. We've been separated for the last six months. Our counselor has suggested light conversations in pleasant surroundings, just to see if we can do it. We can't.

Will's voice prods me, "You said if I let go I could have you. I see that's not true."

"Have me? You'll never get it." Asshole.

"Haven't I stayed away and stopped calling?"

I remember myself locked in the bathroom with him, my arms pinned to the wall. "It's more than your harassment, it's about control. Putting me back in your cage."

He blurts "Fuck you, I'll walk home!" so loud that his bloated face deflates as he jumps back from the table and hobbles away on his injured knee. The other diners look without looking, faces melting with disdain.

I stand and watch him recede, his back rigid, refusing to turn. Then I throw down some bills and drive home dreading a glimpse of him, scared I'll have to pick him up, scared I won't. He leaves a message on my machine, "I give up. Divorce me, bitch."

* * *

When I return to Costa Rica I encounter a mutual friend of Adrian's and mine at the bus station. "Hey Brian, *que pasa?*" It's always great to see one of my few English speaking friends.

He turns, "Happy days, Danielle, nice to see you," stringy blond hair flying as he bounds over with an elfin grin in his signature guise: handmade motley boots, swim trunks barely astride his thin hips and, only because he's in town, a ratty t-shirt. He smacks me on the lips Brit-style. "I'm here to pick up Adrian, but I can't find him."

My heart skips. "Nice coincidence. I just dropped off my holiday visitors on the same bus."

"I'd better go hunt him down before he takes a taxi. He doesn't know I'm here." As he dances away he calls back, "I'm staying at Adrian's for awhile until I get another caretaker's job. Come on up."

I look through the arriving throngs trying to see where

Brian has gone, but can't find either of them. Disappointed, I head home and resolve to drive up and invite them to dinner in the coming week. I remember Adrian's flip offer from over a year ago. Heat radiates from my center. Luck is with me. It's so hard to communicate here in this primitive part of Costa Rica. Although our sleepy seaside village has electricity and public phones, neither has reached us in the mountains yet.

* * *

My heart thuds with fear-laced excitement as I drive up Adrian's mountain road, better suited to horses than cars. At least it's the dry season now so my fear is limited to being rejected romantically and doesn't include sliding off the trail and over a cliff. I've been to Adrian's once with my husband. Oops, not my husband anymore. Can't get used to being single after thirty years. It's been hell for a long time. I'm ready for some heaven.

Adrian hasn't come to Costa Rica alone. He greets me with a big hug, a hearty laugh, and introduces me to his ten-year-old son, Jesse, and Jesse's friend. I invite them all for a swim and dinner the next day.

Down on the river, we slip, slide, laugh and dive off the cliff, spin in the whirlpools, sunbathe on the hot rocks; and when the sun drops behind the mountain we struggle back up to the house.

After eating, the kids are worn out enough to play board games with Brian. I join Adrian on the balcony under the stars. He takes my hand; that small movement ignites a burn that spreads through me. I return the pressure. We turn towards each other and kiss like I haven't been kissed since high school, when kissing was it. But it's not the memory of the past or the promise of the future. It's his plump sweet lips nibbling lightly on mine, tongues touching, hands savoring soft skin.

"You're beautiful," he whispers. "Your smile's so sparkly."

"And your eyes."

I'm done plucking passion from the tree of dreams. I'm free. I can have the real thing; hold it, run my fingers over it, squeeze until my nails puncture its plump skin, the sweet nectar dribbles into my mouth and down my chin.

Fear of Falling

"*Vamonos!*" grins Moreno as he cinches the last of the saddles. He is the Costa Rican equivalent of the Marlboro man, all confident, handsome and strong. The ever present hand-rolled cigarette hangs from the corner of his lips. The five of us mount, depart from Buena Vista Lodge, and head up the Escaleras Mountain towards Cascada Nuayaca, the largest waterfall in Costa Rica. The two hour trek will take us along the ridge and down the other side. Our guide leads us through a spit of primary rainforest, the ocean on one side, valley on the other. Our sure-footed mounts know the way and keep a steady pace as we get used to the feel of animal between our legs.

Adrian and I are showing our young friends Jacob and Van one of our favorite sights in the Southern Zone. After an hour of steep ascent on rocky, slippery trails we need a break. At the crest we dismount. We take in the view, rest our tender backsides and smoke a joint. We gaze seaward on breaking waves cutting over the shore of Punta Dominical, turn 180 degrees to the thick-treed valley below, then continue to our destination singing old cowboy songs to pass the time.

A wave of fear washes over me as the majestic double-tiered falls looms into view. I look up, expecting to see the tree falling on me—the one I didn't see the first time, two years ago, floating in this same pool. It's a gut reaction. My first time back here since the accident. I remember.

* * *

My daughter, Guiselle and I had planned a trip to Nuayaca, a last diversion before I returned to the States. Some new friends were meeting us. They were late. A hard day to start early, after a Saturday night's partying. We sipped fresh fruit *refrescas* until they arrived. The sun already high, we were too hot to ride in the back of their truck with Xan, our golden retriever. We decided on separate cars.

"Meet you at the swing bridge," I called. We took the low road. They took the high and had to ford the stream, up to the floorboards, but they made it. We parked our car, crossed the swing bridge, and started the hot trek to the falls, stopping at Lulo's house to ask permission to access his property. Just a formality. This wonderful friendly man and his wife were always happy to pass the time of day with us and offered us refreshment. We took short respite in the shade before the final push.

They waved good bye. *"Buen dia para las cataratas. Nadie esta alla hoy. Tranquilo."* We'd have the place to ourselves. It was summer and there was no rain. The river was low. We descended through the jungle following the increasing crescendo. The falls stunned us; two long cascades, one 150 feet, the other 65 feet tall, spilling into two large *posas*, (pools), one above the other. The spray covered us in cool mist. We slid down the rocks and dove into the icy water laughing, all shivery in our paradise. A couple of the guys climbed a rope up the cliff of water. They disappeared behind the falls, reemerged on an overhang to survey the scene before jumping. Guiselle and I floated around on inner tubes paddling and playing in the water. Feeling the ripple of a breeze high above my head, I raised my eyes. What an enchanted land!

A huge crack shattered the air over the rush of the water. Maybe dynamite or a big gun. Leaves fluttered down from the ridge. Then the sky fell. The sound was deafening. I was swallowed up, submerged by a green giant. I couldn't find my way up or out. Arms of leaves grabbed me, held me under. Vines tangled and twisted round me. I couldn't move or breathe.

Guiselle was in the middle of the pool when she heard the blast. Instinctively, she dove down and away from the crashing, eyes wide open watching bubble trails of broken branches turned to javelins, *bejuco* gourds to bombs, exploding all around her. The trunk of the giant tree catapulted into the pool feet from her. A massive wave knocked her to the rocks near shore. She surfaced screaming, "Mom, Mom, where are you?"

I was struck dumb. Heard her voice, but could only move in slow motion struggling up through the water, leaves, branches and debris to finally suck in fresh air. I yelled, "I'm okay. Oh my God! Are you? What happened?" I emerged from the canopy looking like a forest nymph; leaves, debris, and biting insects covering me from head to toe. No punctures, no slashes. Alive.

Why were we both left untouched as broken branches became lances and tree trunks turned to battering rams falling all around us? Coincidence, luck, fate? It was not the time to ponder such philosophical questions. We were in shock. How could we have been in the wrong place, at the wrong time?

* * *

Now I think back to what had transpired in the last two years and begin to answer the questions. I took no risk that day, but I just happened to be in the very right place at the very right time, not the other way around. My marriage had been foundering. I'd tried everything to save it, to the point of losing my self. I made the break. The divorce was hard and learning to live alone after thirty years was even harder.

Then Adrian came into my life, a handsome curly-haired mountain man. A loner.

I found sensuality. It overtook me. I still wasn't independent. All I wanted to do was be with him. He was not so overcome. He wasn't interested in a committed relationship if that meant more than a few weeks together per year. "I'll see you when I'm in Costa Rica, and we'll get together for some vacations," was all he could offer. I thought I could change him. I had lots to learn. About independence and taking risks. Hiding in my house because I was afraid another tree was going to fall on me, was not the way to go. That tree cracked me wide open. I wanted to keep it that way.

* * *

Because there is such a thing as a second chance, my memory gives the scene a mystic aura. I can feel every curve and point of rocks beneath my feet. The mist softens my face. The intense sounds become symphony. The sun-drenched cascades are glistening diamonds.

Young Jacob, long hair pulled back into a ponytail, slim hips barely holding up his surfing trunks, dives into the pool, swims to the edge of the falls, and begins climbing the rocks through the thick white lace. He urges me over to join him. "Come climb with me, Danielle."

I'm still in pretty good shape for my age and he knows I like adventure. I look back at Adrian. He shrugs smiling, "Not me. I've got a kid to get through school," and waves me on. I dive in and swim to the cliff of cascading water. Look up at Jacob about 20 feet above me.

"Come on up," he says. "You can do it. It's such a high!"

"How'd you get up there?" I hesitate.

"Easy. Just step up on these rocks. They're not slippery."

I look up to the first plateau of the falls behind me to the safety of shore. I turn my back on it. Gulp air. One step. Another. Jacob holds out his hand. I don't look down. The vertical rock stairs are almost higher than my legs can reach. I pull myself up. Take another step. I grab his hand to reach the plateau. My sturdy mountain-pony legs keep me steady. I rest. Sit with my back to the rocks. My friends look small in front of me. I feel big. Big with the pounding of my heart. Big with my eyes on the falls.

Jacob is my leader. I watch him climb to the next level and wait. I follow him. The next flight is easier. I do it alone. Reach the second plateau and the edge of the falling water. Again I look back and realize I can't go back the way I came. Holy shit! Maybe I'm crazy. I look past the edge behind the falls. There's the passageway. Enough room to sit knees up. I look through the roaring sheets of water distorting the view to an eerie softness. Another moment to rest. Don't want the inertia of fear to stop me.

The last ascent is the steepest and most difficult. Jacob eggs me on. I stand above it all. Fear is now exhilaration. Thousands of fire hoses on full force erupt below my feet. I'm so small. So high. So vulnerable. So excited. So afraid to jump. There's no going back.

"Yeah Danielle, you did it! Jacob cheers, "The hard part is over." He sweeps leaves off the promontory and prepares to jump.

"Wait! Don't leave me up here alone. I want to go first." I yell over the roar. "What do I do?"

"Jump out as far as you can. Don't stiffen up. You'll be under for a while, but you'll pop up."

It's time. I step to the edge, survey the scene from my slight foothold midway up the falls. Water crashes below me. I inhale, exhale huge clots of fear. Somehow I loosen the grip my feet have made with the rocks. And jump!

I fly, hang, drop through the air screaming, arms outstretched. "Aiyee!" I smash through the foaming barrier, shoot to the bottom. Stop. Reverse direction. Finally pop to the surface gasping. Ecstatic. Unconquered. Alive!

My Friend George

An innocent looking mosquito bites me behind the knee. No big deal. Where I live in the tropics of Costa Rica I'm used to all kinds of creatures. Snakes, chiggers, mosquitoes, fungi—are all acceptable tradeoffs for the beauty and wildness of the rainforest. I return to Florida and my job, and forget about the lesion; a small bump, out of sight. A month passes. I begin to feel something. Not an itch, not a pain, just a light tingling. I take a look. Man, I thought that was a mosquito bite, but it's still there. A little cysty thing. Worry flickers through my mind, but I'm too busy to dwell on it.

I've been going to a homeopathic doctor trying to find the source of my migraines. I've tried almost everything else with no success. He tests me using a weird electrical body-scanning device and can detect parasites. While lying supine on the table, something makes me ask him to check the bump on the back of my leg. He palpates, even squeezes it, then shrugs, "Just a cyst. No head. It'll probably just dissolve. Don't worry about it." Okay, I won't. It's just that the tingling sensation is getttting more frequent and irritating.

Life goes on. I'm working with a biologist from Mote Marine Laboratories taking the mobile touch tank and aquarium to schools in the area. We exchange stories of life in the tropics. He mentions the botfly. "How gross!" he grimaces. "The egg is injected into a mammal, grows into the larval stage and after about six weeks, pops out and flies away."

"Oh yeah," I remember. "Even humans have them. Our caretaker gets them from working around the animals. They're really hard to get out if they're not ready."

Instantly a fiery rush of adrenaline washes through my body exiting through my scalp and fingertips like a bolt of lightening. Oh my God! Could that be what's in me? My heart races, sweat breaks out on my upper lip. I'm too shocked and embarrassed to bring it up or check it out in front of him. I wait endlessly to get home, race to a well-lighted window, and twist my body around to get a really good look at the cyst. A little hole has appeared in the center. While I scrutinize it, a tiny tube pokes out of the hole and retreats. I scream, aghast. It's the breathing spiracle of the botfly larva. A loathsome creature is living inside me and eating my flesh! This is a horror film come true.

For the last month my subconscious would not let me consider the possibility of a maggot subsisting on my tender tissue. Now I have no choice but to deal. One little larva parasitizing my gigantic body has not killed me and is not going to, but the thought of it might make me go insane. I've got to stop thinking of this subjectively. I have choices. I can run around screaming and tearing at my flesh like in the movies, or I can look at a logical method of removal. Short of waiting for nature to take its course—at least another two weeks, which I really can't abide—what other options do I have?

I can try pulling it out. I call my scientist friends hoping they'll be more interested than disgusted by the problem. They're excited by the challenge. We set up an operating stage on the floor of the dining room with bright lights, alcohol, tweezers and a magnifying glass.

I lie on my stomach. "I can't see."

Candy, holding the glass, says "Sorry, you can't. You have to be completely still or we'll never be able to get it."

"Ready?" asks Mara, the invertebrate specialist with the tweezers.

"Ready." I grit my teeth, clench my jaw.

Each time the tube emerges Mara grabs it, but when she pulls she gets no purchase. "Damn. It won't work. Something's holding it." We give up. Though disappointed I'm still not ready for the knife. I can turn this into a hands-on, chance-of-a-lifetime science experiment. I need to research.

This variety of botfly (*Dermatobia hominis*) uses not only the human species as a host, but birds and mammals, as well. If there are enough of the larvae they can actually kill the host, but usually the relationship is one-on-one and more cooperative than parasitic. They just need room and board until they're ready to spread their wings and fly away. As mine grows the tingling feeling I experience becomes a biting one. It usually happens in bed and feels like tiny hot needles searing me from the inside out.

What about infection? Not to worry. Each botfly maggot

secretes an antibiotic into its hiding place to prevent other microscopic organisms from ruining dinner. They carry their own antiseptic, but no pain killer or tranquilizer.

I find out that there was no way my fat hairy grub was going to squeeze through that tiny breathing hole. The larva has two anal hooks that hold it securely in position. If it is pulled on, the hooks sink deeper into the flesh as its survival instinct kicks in.

In the *campo*, (countryside) where the *torsalo*, (botfly) still flourishes, there are several recommended ways of extracting them. The meat treatment involves placing a thick slab of raw meat over the hole, effectively cutting off the air from the breathing spiracle and causing the larva to vacate its den and burrow up through the meat in search of air. I can't see strapping a piece of raw beef to my leg in the general course of my day, so I choose the less primitive form of this cure, using Vaseline as an alternative. It seems my little fella knows how to hold his breath. Another failure.

Another week passes. I am meeting my daughter in Martha's Vineyard for a vacation. She'll know what to do. She's lived in the Costa Rican rainforest for several years. Though the feeding is becoming more intense, like getting a mini tattoo from the inside, I decide I can wait a little longer.

Guiselle knows another method of extraction also learned from the caretaker. This time I stand up. She lights a long sturdy kitchen match, throws it into a narrow glass and suctions it quickly onto my leg. The oxygen-eating flame is supposed to form a vacuum in the glass causing the maggot to pop right out. But again no luck This guy hangs tough.

I'm finally getting used to my little hanger-on. I name it

George, in honor of our feisty president; digging in his hooks when things get hard, thwarting all efforts of removal. Now that the horror has worn off I find diversion from my revulsion by creeping out my friends and family. The farther north I go the more freaked out people are about my freeloader.

"Wanna see my new pet?"

"I don't see anything."

"Look. See George peek out and wag hello?"

"Oh shit! That's disgusting."

They can't understand why I haven't been to a doctor.

The scalpel is my last resort. Not only is it the most invasive method, it'll be hard to find a doctor who will take me seriously and know what to do. I return to Florida and contact my old friend from Infectious Diseases, Dr. Vera. She cut out a deep staph infection contracted on my last excursion to the tropics. She'll know what to do. But because of the extra-specialized division of labor in our medical system, she sends me to a surgeon.

I explain the situation and after a cursory exam George fails to make an appearance. With some skepticism the doctor shrugs, "Okay let's do an exploratory."

I lie on the examination table while the nurse swabs me down. "This is a new one for me," she says. The doctor, still not having seen the parasite, numbs the area and slices across its center. The nurse's face juts closer and with a quick intake of breath, I hear, "Jesus!"

The doctor thrusts her fingers into the opening and pulls out the plump, hairy, squirming grub. "Got the little fucker!" rolls off her tongue. I turn to her sheepish smile.

"Oops. Sorry." she says, "but I've never seen anything like this before. This'll liven up my dinner party talk for weeks to come."

I laugh, "You didn't believe me, did you?"

She shrugs with a side-mouthed grin.

George is still alive and not happy. His fat body—about the size of the tip of my finger—curls and uncurls, hair bristling, as the nurse prepares him for the lab. "This is the most interesting day I've had here in the last three years. All we usually see are those boring heart surgeries."

The Last Resort

Candy, Matt and I pack my Nissan Patrol and begin our drive south to the Osa Peninsula, the last frontier in Costa Rica. The road's better than it used to be, but even when it turns slick and pot-holey with rain, we've got the best little tank of a four-wheel drive ever made. At least that's what everyone said when I bought the Patrol. I moved to Costa Rica part-time to be closer to my daughter. Candy and Matt are two of my oldest and best friends, and they've finally made good on their threat to meet me here for an adventure in the wild: isolated beaches, primeval forests, vast monkey-filled jungles buzzed by flocks of tropical birds. Whatever we meet up with will be spicily exotic after the bland over-developed flatness of our Florida homes.

Driving the Pacific Coast Highway, the tall craggy cliffs hang over crashing waves and settle down into flat expanses of giant mangroves and wide deltas. We turn inland onto the Osa

Peninsula, when, Screech-Bang-Clang-Screech, the car totally seizes up.

"You've got to go for help, Danielle," says Candy. "I'll go with you, and Matt can stay behind with the car."

I know Spanish, but Matt knows mechanics. We stand on the side of the road scanning up and down until a bus rounds the corner. I flag it down and we jump on. "We'll get off at La Palma," I yell, watching Matt's uneasy smile recede in a cloud of black fumes.

Shortly the bus driver stops and points, "La Palma."

"Muchas gracias." I thank him and turn to ask a local about a mechanic.

"Si, hay dos acruzar de la calle. Vea, el rotulo Taller El Ceibo?" The friendly *Tico* (diminutive for Costa Rican) points to a rudimentary sign above a primitive garage. Two guys are working on a car up on concrete blocks in a clutter of black greasy tools.

"Hola, tiene un mechanico?" I hesitate. *"Y un camion*—uh." What do you call a tow truck in Spanish? We need a tow truck before anybody can fix anything. I've got to be kidding if I think there's such a vehicle anywhere close to this small dusty village. I get a *'si'* on the former, but a 'no' with an unknowing shrug on the latter.

Candy hangs back nervously looking around, and spots Matt, his 6' 4" frame stuffed into the front seat of a vegetable truck with two men, followed by the Patrol tied to the back bumper with a frayed rope. "My God, how'd you get here so fast?"

He smiles and pats his new *amigo* on the back. "The first car I waved to, stopped. Can you believe it? They jumped right out to help, stuck their heads under the hood, saw it wasn't a side-of-the-road job, and using signs, offered me a tow into town."

A mechanic saunters over wiping his oily black hands on even dirtier pants. Though my car-mechanic Spanish is not good, the car is finally situated over a dark square hole in the ground and the hood opened. While waiting in the sweltering sun we scan the lot for a bit of shade. Not a tree, branch or leaf in sight. Just a pole, topped by a crude sign announcing the garage and a picture of the tallest tree in the jungle, *el ceibo*, the magnificent kapok tree. The joke's on us. Jungle? This is a desert. A dry, hot, dusty one.

"It's the clutch," one comes over to say.

"Can you fix it?"

"*Claro que si.*" he nods smiling. "All we need is the part."

"Where's the part?"

"You must go to Puerto Jimenez. Maybe two hours down the road."

"We have to go? *Que lastima!* Can you at least call to see if they have it?" My *gringa* impatience starts to show.

"*Bueno* okay. I will walk to the phone in the square in a little time. When I finish the other job," the mechanic says.

What's a little time? Maybe forty or fifty minutes? This *Tico* time thing works both ways. We are reminded there's only one phone per village in these primitive areas.

"Everything'll be all right. I'm sure it can be fixed," soothes Candy smiling at the mechanic, who's smiling back, ogling this good looking blond gringa as we walk towards the phone. She is what her mother named her; tight spun sugar curls fly off her head, delicate blue eyes and soft pink skin. Her favorite colors. Her smile says 'sweet', her demeanor says 'take care of me', and men flock around her.

After a rapid unintelligible conversation on the phone the mechanic turns. "They will fly it in from San Jose to the parts store in Puerto Jimenez tomorrow."

"Huh? Fly from San Jose?" I'm discouraged. Hardly anyone carries parts for a Nissan Patrol, an obscure model built in Spain. A trickle of worry dribbles into my consciousness. We have only a week down here before we must return for my daughter's engagement party. I'm getting edgy, and it's getting late.

We ask about lodging. A taxi takes us to the only accommodations in the area on a little backwater bay at Playa Blanca. "Hey this ain't bad considering our predicament," says Matt as we walk through an open-air restaurant and bar and look through swaying palm trees to the water's edge. The *duena* shows us the only room, set behind the bar. It has three beds so crammed together that to get to the farthest you have to climb over the closest. Each bed is covered with a different faded but clean flowered spread. In the corner is a 'private' bath. Instead of a door, a thigh-high floral plastic shower curtain hung on a rope covers the opening. More floral curtains, similarly rope-hung, droop over the only window looking out on a huge sow rooting around in the backyard. All the flowers give it a certain country charm and it is right on a beach.

Thirsty and hungry, we return to the restaurant and take a table overlooking the Gulf. Zeidi, owner, cook and waitress, suggests the whole fish with rice and beans. We all immediately nod, having spied the fishing *pangas* awaiting the next high tide. Salsa music plays in the background as she arrives with huge delectable platters of red snapper, their backs slashed for quick even cooking. Heads with glassy eyes peek out from the rice, beans and salad. The plates, garnished with *mandarinas* (sour oranges) could be a 16th century still life.

"You will want to attend the party tonight," Zeidi says.

"*Que pasa?*" Matt asks with one of the only Spanish phrases he's learned so far.

"*El cumpleanos de mi hermano.* My brother's birthday. There will be much dancing."

Matt's big handsome face has grown a bit long with age, as his belly has grown wide, but he's kept his youthful love of women and life. "I can't do that crazy fast-stepped stuff, but I like to watch. The women in your country are very beautiful." His large laugh reveals a pornographic mind and a charming sense of humor. I translate. Zeidi blushes.

A particularly lively merengue starts playing. "I think I can dance to this one." I jump up and two-step around trying to keep my upper body still while the lower part gyrates. It's difficult, but after two quick beers, I'm loose. I'm always the first one to get up, arrive, speak, laugh, or lose patience. Though I've been coming to Costa Rica for several years, not too much of the lazy pace of Latin life has seeped into me yet.

"*Muy bien!*" laughs Zeidi grabbing Matt's and Candy's arms, "*Vengan.* You two must try also." After a few more beers we're all up shuffling around, laughing foolishly and forgetting our problems. "*Bueno, nos vemos.* We will see you at the fiesta this night."

It's sunset. A great ruckus rings through the palm trees between the restaurant and the shore. A flock of scarlet macaws flushes in a squawking salute—multicolored Chinese kites of red, blue, yellow and black, moving not at all silently across the sky. My friends and I head to our room as a quick dark sets in. The big sow is snuffling around nearby. Matt sticks the key into the rusty lock. The jiggling and twisting alerts the sow to our presence and her curiosity gets the best of her. She saunters over. We scatter. Candy screams, "Watch out! She's gonna trample us."

The key's still stuck in the door. I double over in laughter. "Help! I can't run."

None of us, obviously, are farm bred. Zeidi saves the day, chuckling her way to the door. We follow behind for protection as she easily flips the key.

Too exhausted to think about a party, we climb over each other, fall into our respective beds. What we thought was the beginning of a much needed good night's sleep becomes just a long nap from which I am rudely awakened by booming disco music. It makes the wall pulsate like the tightly pulled skin of a drum. My chest throbs. The beds begin to scoot across the floor. I look around. Candy has the pillow over her head and Matt's gone. I try the pillow trick and fail. Thick anger creeps through my exhaustion. "Goddamn it!" I jump out of bed, throw on some clothes and head for the bar.

The party's in full swing. Matt's sitting at the bar with a big drink and a wide grin. I'm not smiling. He stiffens when he sees me. "Couldn't sleep either," he shrugs sheepishly. "Thought I'd join 'em not fight 'em."

I don't take the hint; holding both hands over my ears I yell at the bartender, *"Basta!* Could you turn that music down!" He looks puzzled, not used to assertive, crabby *gringas*. He complies. Now embarassed I thank him and shrink back to the room. Matt reluctantly follows.

In the morning a taxi takes us to Puerto Jimenez. Dropped

at the parts shop, we find out that the clutch hasn't arrived. "Tomorrow it will come, *por supuesto. No problema.*"

Puerto Jimenez is an old mining town on the Osa Peninsula and not a resort area. We *gringos* are told there are a couple of hotels on a strip of beach on the Golfo Dulce. A taxi drops us off at the one called The Last Resort. *"Espera, por favor."* I ask him to wait. "There's no one around. Is it open?"

A down-at-the-heels, expatriate American couple appears from around the corner. "Oh yes, we are," the wife says as she tries to plump up her stringy grey hair.

"It's the rainy season. Not many tourists this time of year." The husband looks irritated to have been disturbed. Doesn't care that his sweaty dingy t-shirt doesn't cover his protruding belly.

Before they show us to a room the man informs us, "There's no electricity. We'll give you candles," he hesitates. "And when you want to flush the toilet or take a shower please let us know."

"Why?" Candy asks.

"Well, we have to turn on the generator." He looks uncomfortably at his wife.

"Turn on the generator to flush the toilet?" Matt's puzzled. "Why aren't you using gravity for the toilet and the generator for some lights?"

The wife looks irritated. "I've been asking him the same question."

He shrugs. "Oh yeah, well, we're working on that."

"You do serve dinner don't you?" Candy asks, looking around at this deserted strip of beach.

"Of course."

"How about showing us our room first?"

Climbing to the second floor of empty rooms overlooking the Gulf, the wife shows us the one next to theirs. "If you need anything we'll be right next door," she smiles, shutting the door behind her.

"Hmm, is this to make their job easier or are they thinking, two gals and a guy in one room. I'll bet they have a peep hole." Matt laughs. "Like in Psycho."

"The Psychokillers," Candy christens them.

After a rest we come down to the candle-lit dining area, sit down, and check out an extensive menu. About halfway through Mrs. Pyschokiller appears and Matt asks about the fish. "No, we're out of that. Ummm, actually, all we have is spaghetti. We weren't able to get supplies."

At least there's a bottle of wine to go with what tastes like Chef Boyardee. We begin to relax, laugh at the crazy day, crack jokes about the strange couple. Matt, who always turns the conversation to sex after a few drinks, comments, "Why don't we give the Psychos what they want? You girls just jump in bed with me tonight."

"Maybe we will, Matt. It might be the only fun we have here." I laugh.

"You can't help being a dirty old man, can you?" Candy rolls her eyes.

"Nope. You know I'm just a horny hermit. Nobody takes me seriously though."

We don't see Mr. Psychokiller lurking in the shadows just out of range of the candlelight, eavesdropping. He makes himself known during our continuing conversation about whether the car part will actually arrive. We jump as his voice filters through the shadows, "It'll never come in one day. Nothin' happens that fast around here." We realize he's heard the earlier part of our conversation. This is creepy. We quickly finish and retire.

My sleep is troubled by nightmares of large pink fish with bulbous eyes leering at us through the peep-holed walls, but morning dawns with all my body parts intact. I sneak out to the beach and dive into the warm water. Suddenly I'm stung all over. Stinging jellyfish. I almost fly to shore slapping and rubbing at my skin. "Ouch, ouch, shit!"

Matt has arrived to see my wild gyrations, with Candy not far behind. Her face is drained of color and she's shaking. "You left me alone in the room with the Psychokillers next door."

"Well I thought I shouldn't let Danielle swim alone."

"I was half dressed, brushing my teeth when I looked in the mirror and saw just eyes peering at me above the windowsill. I screamed and ducked, threw on a robe, checked the hall before I opened the door, and ran like hell."

"Oh my God, Candy!" My stinging forgotten, I hold her until she stops shaking.

"I could've been murdered!"

"Shit! My nightmare's come true. Big fish eyes peering in."

"Let's get the hell out of the 'Last Resort'." No use checking with the police. There're no such force in these primitive areas. We throw our things together and wait for yesterday's taxi out on the road that will take us back to town. Thank God we paid in advance. Our one mutual thought—will they have the clutch? They do.

Will we ever see idyllic beaches, crashing waves and

monkey-filled jungles? Candy's optimism is showing stress cracks. She no longer sees herself frolicking on black volcanic sand beaches. Matt assesses the amount of time it'll take to install a new clutch in less than perfect condition. And I'm in the future counting back. There just aren't enough days left on this trip to find paradise, even if *los mechanicos* are Kryptonite-carrying supermen. My spirits droop. How will I tell my companions it's all over? We'll have to leave as soon as the car is fixed if not before.

The men at *El Ceibo* greet us with smiles and immediately start to work.

"Dos horas no mas."

"Two hours," raising my eyebrows. We wander the streets buying snacks at the *pulperia*, checking out the offerings at the only *tienda*—mostly cheap towels, the ubiquitous blue jeans and plastic housewares—displayed in the manner of a 1950s US Five and Dime. We end up at the *cantina* for a beer. We trudge back through the dusty heat to the *taller*.

Matt and I check on the car. The clutch has been installed and they're ready for a test spin. The car starts. It begins to move forward. Jerks. Something's wrong. It's sputtering, laboring. The driver changes gears. First, second, no more. No power. No speed. No more vacation. No way home.

I go to find Candy. Lying in the dirt behind a rusted out hulk, she has found one of the skinny mange-covered *Tico* dogs that wander the countryside. "Poor thing. It'll be run over if it stays there." She kneels down. "Oh my God! It's almost dead."

The emaciated animal trembles in its death throes. My heart sinks. I grab a guy by the arm, *"El perro esta muriendo."* It's dying. "Can't you do something?"

"*Nada.* There is nothing we are able to do. It will die here or in front of a car. One less is better." He shrugs, "There are too many starving dogs in this country."

Tears spring to my eyes. I walk away. I cry for the dog. I cry for the car. I cry for our ruined vacation. Then I take a deep breath, return and apologize, "I'm so sorry guys. You're always telling me I take too many chances. Now I've included you in this mess."

Matt puts his arms around me. "Hey, it's an adventure, by God."

Candy gives me a big hug, "Even though it's not the one we planned. We're in this together Danielle, and we'll get out of it together."

Matt takes charge, "First let's find out what time the next bus leaves."

"And if we can leave the car here," Candy chimes in.

After waiting and riding. More waiting. More riding. We're back to Cortez—the end of the bus line and only 30 miles from home. The rain pours down from a dark sky. Wet umbrellas reflect the one street light. No taxis. One old pickup. The driver agrees (for a high price) to take us as far as he can go. He has no four wheel drive. We're desperate. We all pile in the front this time. I straddle the gear shift. And Candy sits on Matt. He's happy—at least until his squashed accordioned limbs start whining.

There's been an attitude change. The trip has become a quest. Like climbing Mt. Everest. The rain becomes a *tormenta.* "Come on, bring on more." My fist rises into the air. "We can take it!" Potholes disappear under rivers until the wheels find them. Kaboom! A tire blows.

"Hit us again. We can do this." I've found my stride—and a *cantina* across the road. "Yes!"

After a couple beers, the blowout (an everyday occurrence to a *Tico*) is patched and we're on our way to our last challenge. The mountain. And my house at the top.

"*Derecha!* Turn right." I yell through the roar of the rain. The driver steps on it when he feels the steepness of the grade. "*Vamos rapidamente!*" We pick up speed until the tires pick up mud. Slow to a halt. Start sliding backwards. We climb out, Matt pays the driver who turns down the hill and slithers out of sight.

We're on our own now. "Okay. I'm used to walking this last kilometer. You all take the flashlight. I'll go ahead and bring back the truck."

"You shouldn't walk alone." Matt and Candy agree.

I quash their concern and start trekking, easily distancing myself from them. Their legs are made for cars not mountains. I round the bend into utter blackness. Fear grabs me. This is fer-de-lance country and I can't see where I'm stepping. Thoughts of poisonous snakes make me start singing, "Johnny comes marchin' home again. Hoorah. Hoorah." One step in front of the other. "Summer tiiiiime and the living is eeeeeasy. Fish are jumpin' and the cotton is high." I sing in a high falsetto. The faint outline of the driveway appears in front of me, the rain-shrouded house behind it. I collapse in exhaustion and relief.

Before I go to retrieve my friends with the truck, I hear them coming. Adrenalin pumping fear has kept them right behind me. "We made it!" I hug them.

"Now that was an adventure!" Matt exhales.

"Armchair traveling right here on your balcony sounds great to me." sighs Candy, "watching the crashing waves and the soaring birds."

God's Caveman

Part One

"Sacred Paths? What kind of name is that for a tour company?"

My friend Lise has just been checking out a new organization in San Anselmo, Costa Rica. "It's some religious non-profit group offering spiritual renewal through tours."

I smirk. "The scenery's so beautiful we'll see God?"

"Hey, don't laugh. They need some people to go on a hiking tour to Talamanca—the falls I was telling you about with the caves. Nobody signed up and the leader's already here. A retired monk. They'll let us go for any donation."

"Guess nobody wanted to be saved."

"All the employees are going, too, to add bodies. You don't have to attend the spiritual retreat part if you don't want to."

"Okay. Let's do it."

The group starts out early, first on horseback. As the trail gets steeper and narrower, we walk. It's hard and slow going.

None of us are seasoned backpackers, except Lise, whom I try to emulate, but my muscles scream in resistance. Her elegant body ranges easily back and forth among the hikers like a snowy egret, her small yellow beak-like cap wigwagging as she cultivates new friends. Yesterday's rain has left the trail slippery and potholey. We are surrounded by rainforest giants. Buttressed roots are ready to trip us, tumescent leaves leak water down the backs of our necks. The increasing slope makes us suck in air with our scenery. We're doing penance in advance.

I catch up with our spiritual guide. He's about forty-five, short and stocky, a *Latino*, but speaks perfect English. The rest of us are *Gringos*.

Between ragged breaths I introduce myself, "Hi, I'm Danielle."

"Hi. I'm Adam. Nice to meet you."

"Same. So, what's a retired monk?"

"Well, I felt the need, after twenty years, to get out of the monastery. Something was missing in my life. I wanted to minister to people, not just work on my own salvation."

"I can relate to that. There aren't many people who could stay cooped up meditating for twenty years and not wonder what they're missing."

He ignores the comment, "In the process I met a woman who changed my life."

"I see."

Lise is ahead of me talking to Chuck, a former addict. He's eager to attend the retreat to get a few past sins off his chest. I hear him say, "I've heard this guy gives a good session."

"Like what?" Lise's interested. She's always open to esoteric opportunities and not afraid to experiment.

"Salvation. It's always about salvation, isn't it? And for God's sake I can use it." Sweat unscrews his dark chocolate curls and drips onto his already soaked t-shirt sporting the quote "Come and Be Moved."

The rest are people gone wrong through some form of abuse; thus the group's purpose, turning life's little foibles to faith and fitness.

We reach the last snaking ridge and a flat place to catch our breath before we slide into the grumble of the approaching cataract. I see an apparition; catch up with Lise. She's spotted him too. "Look at that guy."

Framed by massive rock protrusions above and below, a god stands in relief; the sun's illumination keeps the shadow's murky mouth from swallowing him. Shoulder-length black ringlets frame his Roman nose, full lips, piercing eyes.

"Is he for real?" His eyes prick and catch mine like double-edged fish hooks. I break my gaze to stare down his bronzed body: steely smooth-muscled arms, stomach, legs; then back up. He's watching me, waiting. I blush, smile. His face lights up.

Lise elbows me. "He likes you."

"Yea, right. I like him too. Who wouldn't?"

Then we're behind the waterfall, the deluge blocking our sight and sound, slapping us in the face with strong wet fingers to wake us from the dream. But he's still there on the other side.

Now he's busy preparing lunch in a makeshift kitchen. Thick pots of rice and beans steam on portable propane burners. An obscenely bright bowl of fresh fruit stands next to pitchers of *refrescas naturales*, pineapple and mango sieved through a colander, then mixed with sweetened cool water.

Introduced to us as Vicente, this caretaker of the caves continues to glance and smile my way as he serves lunch. I'm caught, slowly reeled in. I approach him speaking Spanish.

"*Hola Vicente, me llama Danielle. Como le va?*"

"*Muy muy bien.*" The grin betrays his pleasure.

"*Que bellisima! Su montana.*"

"*Y tu tambien* (you, too). *Podria mostrarte mas. Hay mas tiempo para descansar despues de almuerzo.*" He'd like to show me around after lunch and he's not wasting any time asking.

I shrug; open my hands in possibility and turn to look for Lise who has disappeared. She'd suggested this hike as a salve for my raw emotions. My relationship is on the rocks. My beau swept away by another. So here's this dark handsome man showing me attention. No matter what will follow, my self-esteem swells.

Vicente sees me searching for Lise. "*Yo la vi. Se fue aya,*" he points down a trail. A sign says 'Danger! Do not enter without a guide'. Of course she did. I'd do the same. That's one reason we get along so well. We're risk takers.

"I will take you." Vicente is proud of his halting English.

God he's beautiful! Shall I throw caution down the falls? "Okay, *vamonos.*" He works here. This is his job.

And the spiel begins. "I saw you as you walked from under the falls. *Que Linda! Que cuerpo!* (So beautiful! What a body!)"

"What a line!" I laugh in English. He doesn't get it. "*Cuantos anos tiene?*"

"*Treinte-cinco.*" (thirty-five)

"That's my son's age."

He doesn't skip a beat. "Are you married?"

"Not anymore."

"*Ah bueno.* I love older women. Forty, *o mas. Perfecto para mi.*"

What if I told him I'm fifty? The twisted sleeves of delight and dread agitate in my gut. I don't think he'd care. His hand reaches out to touch me and plucks instead a startling red passionflower from its twining stem. He holds it out to me. We emerge from the murky closeness of the trail to a Titanic rock spewing the last in a long series of waterfalls into the valley's shocking green mouth. Thick-jawed mountains and patches of sea-glitter surround it.

"This is my home," he sighs. "I have lived here for five years. But now too many tourists come and I must soon reclaim my privacy."

We turn our faces into the cool mist. Lise pops up bare-chested from behind a rock. She's found the pool fed by the falls. "This is heaven! Come on in."

I look questioningly from her to Vicente. She shrugs smiling and waves us in. I gulp. We strip. The bronze Adonis stands before me. I'm shy, embarrassed, exhilarated. I take a quick sidelong glance, a deep breath and dive to meet Lise veiled beneath the rushing water. We hug and shiver and laugh out loud, "This is wild."

Nature has become supernatural, pulsing with energy. Vicente joins our frolicking, but keeps a discreet distance. He doesn't know what to make of these bold gringas, but he doesn't want to ruin his luck. We too are a little nervous to be alone with our nude stranger, We grab the moment in all its perfection, but like water, it slips through our fists and we must return; Vicente to his chores and we to our retreat. I've decided to give it a try.

We are seated in a circle on flat boulders under another smaller overhang. Adam stands to welcomes us. After a brief personal history and introduction, he asks the group, "Are you in pain from past troubles, present abuse? I need a volunteer to show you how my method works."

Chuck jumps right up. "Man, I need help right away. I'll try it."

Adam makes an example of this poor lost soul in order to teach us how to accept ourselves as God does. "All you have to do is tap hard on the top of each of your fingernails in order with your other index finger, then repeat with the other hand and say 'I accept myself. I accept God. I forgive my enemies, my family, everyone that's hurt me." All the time tap-tap-tapping; not just Chuck, but all of us tapping. Then pressing the hole in our hearts. Pressing hard that place that hurts just above and to the left.

Chuck begins to cry as his story erupts. This thirty-year-old rehabbing coke addict, already through his fourth wife, has taken less than fifteen minutes to reach a zealous state. And we have helped. I look around at the others: six barefoot cross-legged cliff dwellers tapping and pressing and shaking their heads. Nobody's laughing, not even Lise. This is not for me, this little missionary ex-monk's workshop. I'm out of here.

Quietly I put on my boots and slip away past the main cave. Vicente is napping on one of the stone sleeping slabs. I do not want to wake him. A solitary hike is what I need. I've had enough heart-pounding experiences for the day, but around the first bend he catches up with me. *"Por favor,* may I guide you? You must see *la madre de cataratas* on the highest ridge. The one from which all the others flow."

Should I be flattered or afraid? I'm both. This young gorgeous Costa Rican drawn to me? My common sense has been sanded away with age, but I go with my instincts. I weigh my certain regret at not jumping at the opportunity with the chance he's a rapist, and hand's down, I agree, *"Si, pero con cuidado,"* I caution. He corrects my accent and gently touches my shoulder to follow him. The trail is easy though steep. We can talk. *"Que raro!* To live and work in a cave."

"I am the caveman of God, *mi corazon.*" He shines, "It is also my e-mail address."

I chuckle. *"Perfecto."*

"I must live in the high jungle. It is what I love. I have only one sister and her family in San Jose. Though I miss them I cannot live there."

"I understand. It's so polluted."

"No solomente eso. I feel so sad there, I cannot live without the jungle. I will take drugs, alcohol, anything to forget." Of course, another addict in rehab.

Spikes of sun flash through a clearing ahead. In it a rusted tin roof settles on weathered boards that range around a red-waxed concrete slab. On the stoop is an old man as weathered as the boards behind him. "I would like you to meet my old friend, Jose. He has lived on this mountain his whole life."

"Hola, Jose. Con mucho gusto." He offers me his hand. In the other is a bunch of bananas.

"Hola, senora. Con mucho gusto. Eat, have a cool drink. It is so hot today."

We rest as he tells me his story. Jose and his family were squatters. They had come over the *Cerro de Muerte* (Mountain of Death) many years ago to carve out a bit of the cloud forest, eking out a living with a few cows and a field of rice and beans. As he had grown older his sons took over the farm. When the land-hungry foreigners had offered them what they thought was a fortune for the poor farm, they succumbed. Now only Jose is left, allowed to live out his life here. I like these *Ticos*. They are gentle, friendly, and strong as oxen. Educated not with books but with experience.

Returning to the trail, forest shadows eat ours. The thick emerald curtain closes over us, muffling the incessant wing-rubbing CRRRRRIIICK of the *chicharras* (cicadas), and the bright calls of birds. It reopens on an eager rush of water over a tall slender cascade, *La Madre*. The pool below billows with her misty skirt-tails.

Vicente silently peels off his clothes. I turn away and take his lead. He asks me to face him. *"Ah mi corazon,* you are so beautiful." He tucks a lock of hair behind my ear and entreats, *"Un besito* (one little kiss), *para un minuto, no mas. Te amo!"*

He loves me? I laugh, shivering wanting to touch him before he vanishes. I invite little bits of kisses, hugs, but I feel nothing. I'm numb. Offered God and love, I take neither and rely on fate.

God's Caveman

Part Two

From my balcony back home, I watch the white hawk scree across the morning sky. A totem to my solitude. I go with it, get high and pick a rune. A little better than newspaper horoscopes, but not as good as dreams, this old Teutonic alphabet fell into disuse after the Middle Ages, but has re-emerged as an oracle for divination. I use it for brain-storming.

I draw Perth. Initiation. The mystery rune points to that which is beyond my frail manipulative powers, symbolized by the flight of the raptor. I am counseled that the old ways have come to an end. It's not the old or the new that's important. It's the now. Is this a sign, a coincidence? Any different than tapping fingers?

The phone rings. I have given Vicente my phone number and e-mail address, cautioning him if one didn't work maybe the other would.

"*Danielle, mi corazon, como estas?*"

"Vicente?" Long pause. I'm nervous. My meager Spanish and a bad connection make it doubly hard to understand him.

"Si."

"*No puedo creer que me llamaste.*" I can't believe he's called.

"*Cuando puedo verte?*" He asks when we can meet again.

I lived through the last experience. "*No se.*" What do I have to lose? I've already lost a bad marriage, a new beau and my fear of living alone. Those were good to shed. What about my life? I just need to be careful and lucky. And to gain? Lusting youth and beauty.

"When will you next be in San Anselmo? I could pick you up and bring you here to see my jungle, my river."

"*Que divertido!* I would love that, but mostly it is you I care to see."

* * *

God's caveman has fallen in love with me. As we walk down the trail into the forest he faces me. His hands cup my cheeks, fingers trace down the rim of my jaw, over my throat, to my shoulders. "*Embrasame. Besame.*" I hold him, graze on his dark lips, learn his ways and words of love. In minutes he offers me his heart, even his hand in marriage. "*Quisiera casarte!*"

"*Que bien,*" Ha ha.

"*No, no senora.* I have loved you from the moment I saw you. I care not for strong drink, drugs or material things, but love, ah, that is a different matter."

He's a man of simple tastes he says. Sleeps with the dark, awakes with the dawn to wander his forests keeping the trails clear, fishing the rivers. Does he think I don't know his history at Sacred Paths? But it's all in the storytelling, this wonderful game. I laugh and go along with it all.

In the distance we see flashes of whitewater falling into transparent pools. He takes my hand and leads me onto the hot flat boulders, into the opening the river has slashed through the jungle. We take off our boots, strip the clothes off our sweaty backs, and dive into the cool water. The river is low, the sun hot above us until the canopy swallows it again.

My skin sizzles like cold water on hot grease. My eyes cut over Vicente's hard brown body and hold his dark gaze. He draws my mouth to his. Rays of adrenalin radiate from my breasts drawing lightning from his fingertips. Burning, racing everywhere. We slither onto the baked rocks. He does things to me that no first-time lover has ever done. I melt as he moves his face between my breasts, draws both my nipples into his full mouth, his tongue giving them equal time. He's found the key. His sweet lips slide lower. My body arches to meet his, joining in jagged pieces of passion.

As we hike back up the hill a residue of gratified desire remains and turns into hunger. Vicente rests under the mango tree, eats a dozen of the golden globes, skin and all. Totally sated he falls asleep under its shade, fulfilling so easily yet another of his primal needs.

I watch him, envying his simple life: acceptance of basic pleasures, avoidance of complexities in the world. It all looks perfect in this moment—no past or future seeping in. But all bubbles must burst. I drive him back into town and drop him off. He must return to his job on the mountain and I to my other life across the water.

He whispers in my ear as we embrace, *"Muchisimas gracias para este dia."*

"Yo tambien." I echo.

"I would like to take you camping to a truly primitive Eden, the jungles of La Amistad, when you return. Would you travel with me, *por favor?*"

"*Si,* but I don't know when I'll be back."

"Send me an e-mail."

"*Por supuesto. Puedo practicar mi espanol.*"

"*Mi querida, te amo.*" He addresses love so easily. His lips discreetly brush my cheek.

"*Hasta pronto.*" I wave as he disappears down the dusty dirt road; that last untranslatable phrase 'until soon', echoing poignantly in the air.

Will I ever see God's cavemen again? It doesn't matter. I've weighed the odds, left fear behind and opened myself to a truly exquisite experience. I will relish the memory of being a part of this beautiful man's life for one extraordinary day.

Getting to Know You–
Humboldt County, CA

Harvest moon full on us. Clear and cold. And it begins with the madrones of marijuana. We oil our hands to keep the sticky hash from becoming flypaper; get the little scissors. Precise, crisp little snip-snips, giving the big first buds, monkey-balls, a nice haircut; protecting it as we snap off the big leaves. I sit with the pickers, listening, watching, learning. The first cutting can earn them in one day what they'd get at McDonald's in a year. Just keep the pipe lit and passing, the beer flowing and the music playing.

Adrian jumps up and out to the balcony with binoculars before I even register the sound of helicopters thump-thumping overhead. "There's no smoke," his face hardens.

Here in Humboldt County, California fall brings high fire danger and the most important event of the year on Harper Mountain—the marijuana harvest. So if it's not a fire, it's a bust. I've heard the stories. Fear knots my stomach. Adrian's paranoia has already sent him to the bathroom as the fight-or-flight syndrome kicks in. The helicopters circle and circle above a small valley maybe a mile from us as the crow flies. Then they're gone. The quiet settles with the dust. Our uncertain inertia mutates into frantic activity. He jumps into the truck, "I'll be back."

"I'm not staying here alone!" I jump in after him. He doesn't argue. I've been invited to this year's harvest knowing the risks. After many winters of living next door to this man in Costa Rica, having our on-again, off-again relationship, I want to know what kind of life he leads in his other home in California. Now I know why it has taken so long to be asked.

The going is slow. The tires kick up so much dust on the dirt road that we can barely see the curves. Sirens burst out behind us. Adrian yanks the car to the side, jams on the brakes. Adrenalin pumps needles through my body, my heart. A stagnant prayer punctures my brain, as it does in times of great fear, breathing life into old childhood habits. "Please, dear God, let them pass." They do.

One after another, three squad cars wail by. Adrian takes his still shaking foot off the brake, gulps a huge breath, and releases it. "Holy shit! They're not chasing me, but I've got to find out what's going on." The threat of danger ensconced in his life is more than I bargained for.

Adrian squeals off after the squad cars, thrilled to be chasing instead of being chased, careening blindly around the curves until we see dust clouds mushrooming ahead. To the left is a smashed gate. The police cars must have turned in. We stop outside the gate. When the dust clears all the doors are open with cops behind them, guns ready and pointed at two of the neighbors lying face down on the ground.

"Keep your heads down!" the lead cop gestures with his gun.

"We're not the ones you want." Mark, Adrian's closest neighbor, gestures. "We called you."

"Don't move!"

"The real thieves—black guys—are getting away. Three cars of them."

After quickly relating the story to the cops, Mark hurries on, "These black thugs came up from the ghetto in San Francisco. They're related to a guy who stills owns property up here and they have a key to the first locked gate. That's how they got in."

Sam adds, "They've got a video camera. Taped the whole thing. You'd better hurry."

After a quick call, the cop on the radio nods. The helicopter must have spotted the thugs leaving. "You'd better be right. And go home in case we need you." They screech off, sirens blaring. Adrian and I help the neighbors up and get the rest of the story.

* * *

All the Harper Mountain growers take eight-hour shifts during the harvest. Mark and Sam, on duty as harvest patrols, have found the broken gate at the entrance to Ray's property. They radio other growers for support, then turn in to take a look. Around the curve three strange cars have pulled in as close as possible to one of Ray's 24-plant patches, doors wide open. The first car is stashed with mature marijuana plants cut off at the stem; or rather the trunk, they're that big. Two young men stand watch wearing black stocking caps and graffiti-covered sleeveless t-shirts flaunting a San Francisco inner city gang insignia. Their bulging black arms plastered with even blacker tattoos hold AK7 rifles. Three more of the group drag plants as big as young trees to fill the next car. One of them spots Mark and Sam, "Freeze mufuckas!"

They hoist their hands high. "We're unarmed. We live around here."

"Don't shoot! We found the broken gate. We're just checking on our neighbor's property."

The law of the mountain decrees no guns. Mark and Sam know better than to be armed. They're trying to uphold the very shaky law—Proposition 215—passed in 1996. That year California passed the Compassionate Use Act, giving medical doctors the authority to write pot prescriptions "for any illness for which marijuana would provide relief." Not only does this make becoming a member of one of San Francisco's pot clubs legal, but the growers line up every year in their little mountain towns to renew their prescriptions, not only for the common pot-associated illnesses of glaucoma, cancer and AIDS but, since 2004, more nebulous ailments: anxiety, Ambient and Valium side effects, headaches.

The prescription gives them the right to plant a crop of 24 plants legally in California. The federal law disagrees. Local cops have the Feds on their backs, but the sheriff wants to be re-elected and knows who pays the bills in Humboldt County. These farmers know their rights. They've caught city boys breaking, entering, trespassing and stealing a 'legal' crop. And to top things off, they saw that one of this gang has a video camera proudly shooting the whole heist while the other guys laughed and clowned around.

Mark has taken the offensive, "We've already alerted other neighbors. They're on the way. I wouldn't do anything stupid—like shoot us."

The gun-toting leader yells, "Thas a mufuckin' lie. You the fuckin' stupid ones."

"If you take those plants out of your cars now and leave the way you came, we won't call the cops."

"Bullshit! My family owns this land and we're takin' what's rightfully ours. Now get the fuck outta here before we shoot ya!"

Mark takes a chance. "You're wrong. This is Ray Trainer's property and you're trespassing."

The gang shuffles around nervously. The leader nods his head towards the cars. "We got most it. Les get the hell outta here."

* * *

We get the call from Mark through the mountain grapevine, "They got 'em and all their stash."

"What happened?"

"They found the camera. It was all there in living color just like we said."

"Lucky for us, they were so stupid." Adrian laughs, "I'll sure be glad when this season's over."

On my last day we drive down Adrian's dusty mountain road and into the redwood forest. We walk in and are instantly surrounded by the majestic trees, wide as houses, tall as skyscrapers, old as Jesus. Now we're the size of voles at the hems of their ancient skirts, lost in the constant haze.

Like the haze of dope: eating it, smelling it, inhaling it,

scraping it off the bottoms of our feet, finding leaves in our pockets and stuck in our hair; a green film of resin settling on and into everything.

I breathe in fresh air to clear my mind, turn to Adrian and sigh, "What's California like in the spring?"

Puppy Love

After living our separate lives in the United States for much of the year, Adrian and I rendezvous in Costa Rica for the season. We have our homes just one mountain away from each other, but frequently share our days, meals, beds and entertainment. We're in love, but keep it part time.

A raggedy-looking dog wanders in while we're drinking coffee on Adrian's patio one morning, droopy dugs swinging as she walks. She has the color and wiry thinness of a Doberman, but her legs are too short. Long in face, ears bigger than her head, eyes bulging behind her nose, she looks more like a rat than a mutt.

"Why where did you come from, Mama? You looking for food? And your pups? Where are they?" She cowers at the sound of Adrian's voice and looks for quick escape.

"Come on, I'm not gonna hurt you." He squats down to make his tall athletic form less imposing, and reaches out to pet her trembling back. "Let me find you something to eat, you skinny little thing."

"Let me try," I say rubbing the back of her head. "She's all skin and bones, poor thing," My voice and touch sooth her while Adrian brings her some leftovers. She devours the food and slinks off.

During the following week she returns each day to be lavished with delicious tidbits, kind words, gentle petting. Each day she stays a little longer. By day four she's basically living there but no puppies have appeared. She's still skinny.

I stop in for coffee. Giving him a hug I ask, "So how're you and mama doing? Don't you think it's time to give her a name?"

"If I name her I'll have to keep her," Adrian says, looking a bit guilty. "I don't want one of these pathetic yappy dogs tripping me up and peeing on everything. I can't anyway," he excuses himself, "I'm leaving soon."

"I hear that new vet, Fernando, will take strays and find homes for them," I say.

"I need to take her there anyway to get her milk dried up. We'll never know what happened to the pups.

In less than a week after the procedure, the dog has wandered into the jungle and returned trailing three puppies that she can no longer feed. Weaned by default, they are old enough and lucky enough to have survived this far. Mama's way smarter than she's beautiful and knows a savior when she sees one.

I've brought my six-year-old grandson Diego over to play with the puppies. One looks like her bug-eyed ratty mom, the large male is champagne brown in soft white socks, but it's the furry black girl in white boots, white blaze above her sweet black face that both he and Adrian fall in love with.

Diego's face lights with angelic joy at the sight of them as he picks up the black one and cuddles her. I laugh with them as they all romp on the floor together, my dog-loving guy, a skinny livewire kid, and three tiny fluffballs. When it's time to go home Diego grabs the little blaze. "I want this one. I'm calling her Fluffy."

"That wouldn't work," I laugh. "Since you call me Fufi," (his take on grandma), "if you name her Fluffy, neither of us will know who you were calling."

"Then how about Sunshine?"

Adrian grins. "Well, I think I'm going to keep one after all. How about this, buddy? If it's okay with your grandmother, the two of you could take care of Sunshine for me until I get back from California."

Diego leaps into the air, corn-silk hair an electrified crown, yelling, "Yes, yes, yes!" with his whole body. He's smitten the way children are—giving total love, receiving total joy. "I'll feed her and play with her all day long." Old enough to know that if he keeps this pup he must take some responsibility for her.

They both look at me. I hesitate, then nod. I already have three dogs, including the car-chasing Lucy, that Adrian has agreed over and over again to take, but never has.

After watching Diego's joy, I see him wavering. How could he possibly take the pup away from this kid? Rolling his eyes at me he says, "Okay, I'll take Lucy in trade when I come back," knowing it would break my grandson's heart to give up Sunshine when he returned. "But will you share her with me when I come back?"

"Yes, yes, yes!" Diego repeats. "I'll let you play with us whenever you want."

On his way back to the United States Adrian clicks off a quickie e-mail from the airplane.

> Oh, Danielle darling, I miss you and the puppy so much. Diego too. While I wing away, watching a penguin surfer movie without sound, my thoughts meander to you and the smell of puppy in your hair. I know I have lost her to Diego in exchange for Lucy. I WAS HER FIRST LOVE, YOU KNOW! I took the whole litter in my lap and leaned over them, warming them from above and below. Sunshine was always my favorite. They're all gone now except little Sunshine. You have her all to yourself until Friday when Diego comes back. I wish that I could be with you for the morning frenzy. Adrian

Diego's family lives in the city during the week for work and school, then returns to my house for surf weekends. He's not happy that I'll have Sunshine longer than he will, but reconciled that weekends are better than nothing. That leaves me with the training, but I've fallen in love with the little fluffball. Adrian has already paper-trained her. She's not yippy, sleeps a lot in my arms, plays daintily, and feels so damn good.

I set up a little bed for her outside on the balcony, but separated from the three other dogs by a bamboo fence. They've all met, but need a little more daytime bonding before I throw her into the pack. She wakes up sometime during the night, realizes she's alone in an unfamiliar place, finds the door to my bedroom and starts whining. Sunshine has gotten used to snuggling with her family. Ignoring her doesn't work. I get up, put her out with the other dogs to sink or swim. She immediately shuts up. I watch for a minute. They sniff each other and settle down together—her new surrogate family.

At daybreak I open the big doors and she's back in the house. Small enough to enter at will through the bamboo slats, she eats up the human attention and her extra puppy breakfast then exits for the more rough-and tumble of a dog's life. The big dogs, Mata and Jake and little Lucy, accept her into the pack. Sunshine explores the dogs, the house and yard: chasing the ball, sniffing the corners, sliding on the slick tiles of the balcony. After assuaging the itch of her erupting teeth on the chewy electric cords, she flops under my chair for a long nap.

At dinnertime Jake waits by the front door where he eats. Lucy's under the house. Her main interest is car-chasing, not food. Sunshine's hanging out with Mata on the kitchen balcony where he and Lucy get fed. Sunshine will eat in the house separated from the other dogs until she learns the pecking order. I whistle a little tune as I stir up a combo of rice, scraps and dog food in their bowls, thinking what fun it is to have a new puppy in the house. But the dogs know the sound of that spoon.

A sharp predatory roar shocks my heart. The loud crack of breaking bones and a screeching yelp makes it pound. Then silence. "Oh my God!" I fall over myself racing for the open door. Mata sits totally silent on his haunches. My eyes follow his to Sunshine, lying like a discarded rag doll on the tile.

"Noooo!" I scream. She is in her death throes. Her neck is twisted at an impossible angle, the gash spewing more blood than any puppy could have. Her little paws twitch in the air. I grab her for the last few jerks. Then it's over. No heartbeat.

Neck slashed and broken, the expanding puddle of blood already coagulating as it drains off the balcony. I hug her to me, wailing, pacing, horrified.

"Jesus Christ! What the fuck!! I raise my fist and scream at him, "You murderer! What's wrong with you?" Mata just sits there, head cocked to the side, so innocent. I've lost a baby, a sweet furry cuddly one that we'd all immediately loved.

Oh Diego, you're going to be devastated. This is nothing like your favorite Animal Planet predator/prey sequence of a scratchy rat becoming a snake's meal. Sunshine is your own baby that sleeps in your arms and warms your soul.

I wrap her still-warm body in soft India gauze, the green colors scarlet with her blood. I must bury her quickly. This is the tropics. If the scavengers don't get her the ants will. I find Diego's bug-collecting shoebox, tuck her in, get the shovel out of the *bodega*, and head for the pet cemetery. The still-fresh grave of our last cat, Brisa, makes digging easy. There'll be no marker. This story is best altered for my soft-hearted grandson, the truth being way too ugly.

I call my daughter Guiselle, voice cracking. "Mata killed Sunshine! I'm so sorry. It was a horrible accident."

"Oh my God! What happened?" she asks.

I tell her quickly. "How are we going to break the news to Diego?" It's Tuesday. They'll drive him back to my place on Friday for the weekend. Sunshine's disappearance will be hard enough for him to stomach without making Mata the killer.

We agree to save him from the anger he would feel for Mata by telling him a lie. "Tell him the puppy disappeared. Give him a little time to digest the news. He's going to be crushed." Tears clog my voice. I hang up and write the dreaded e-mail to Adrian:

Dearest Adrian,

I'm so sad. Mata killed the puppy yesterday right in front of my eyes. I guess it was because of food. His mean streak is getting worse. Thank God it was instantaneous. Quickly slit and broke her neck. Diego doesn't know yet. I cry for him. It's made me think about life—so quick, so short, so unpredictable. We're going to have Mata fixed asap. I miss you already. Little Sunshine too. Life's lessons are sometimes very hard. I love you, Danielle

My heart is in my throat as Guiselle turns up the driveway on Friday. The car door opens and Diego stands before me, eyes cutting into mine, "What d'you mean, Fufi, you can't find Sunshine?" his face full of reproach.

"I'm so terribly sorry, Diego. Maybe she'll find her way back," I stutter.

Diego starts to wail, "My puppy, my Sunshine, she has to come back. Oh no, she can't be lost. I just got her. I love her too much."

The sorrow on his face is a stake through my heart. Of course I can't hold back my tears either. Looking at Guiselle's and my sad faces, his shoulders droop. He turns and climbs the stairs not even asking if we can hunt for her.

Without conviction Guiselle calls up to him, "We can get you another puppy."

He doesn't react or answer and goes off to his room alone. I cry for him.

Adrian hasn't answered my e-mail. I knew he'd be upset remembering his last e-mail intertwining his love for me with that of Sunshine. I call him, figuring I owe him that. "Adrian?"

Nothing. Finally. "Yea."

"I wanted to talk to you. I know how hard it is to lose that pup."

"Yea?"

"It was horrible! To see her killed like that in front of my eyes. And by Mata."

"One day. She lasted only one day in your care."

"What? You're blaming me? You know it wasn't my fault. It just happened."

Silence on the other end confirms the accusation.

"Obviously, this isn't a good time to talk."

"No."

"Okay. E-mail me when you're feeling better. Bye." Why'd I say that? Why does it still take me so long to react, assess, and respond? So I wait. Two weeks later I receive his e-mail.

> I feel like writing a little today. I am still upset the pup only lasted a day in your care. It was all too fresh. I bonded with the jungle pups, loved them, remembered them needing me, the feel of fur, smell, all of it. The morning after getting your message I took your photo off the fridge and ripped it into pieces. My horoscope said lay off the send button. Used the anger to do work. Sorry doll, but I was depressed. Gloomy weather. The economy tanking. The Republicans looting us more than normal at the end of their term. But now I'm feeling better and forgive you for whatever. My return is Apr 3rd. Love, Adrian

He *forgives* me? Asshole. He thinks highly of himself, a positive trait, but when depressed, only of himself. When things get tough, he's simply not there. I've learned independence and like my time alone to read, dance, laugh, fart, scream out loud, or just stare into space, but this is going too far. I'm pissed. If this is the e-mail he sent, how hurtful was the one he didn't send? Tore up my photo? I take his lead and furiously start typing a reply. Don't know if I'll send it, but at least it'll vent my own anger and hurt. Each day I embellish, add and subtract, as I think of more ways to skewer him. It makes me feel better just to get it out, but I lay off the send button.

His silence gives me time to think. While listening to Odetta sing "Can't Afford To Lose My Man" it all becomes clear. Yes, I can afford to lose him. I've let fear overcome my well-being and freedom. It's time to prune that thing called love. Time to take the risk. Either the roots will die or it will sprout in a new form.

When Adrian returns to Costa Rica he calls to tell me he'll meet me at the farmers' market—a very public place—and he can't wait to see me. He greets me with, "Hi doll, I've missed you," as if nothing has happened.

On the contrary, I'm bubbling over with confrontation. I half smile and wait until we walk to the car. "I know you get into these funks. I'm so sorry this happened, but you know, I bonded with that little Sunshine too. Cuddled her close, felt her warm nose tickling my hand."

"I forgave you."

"Forgave me? For what? For taking on a fourth dog? For keeping an eye on her? For losing sleep when she whined and whined in the night to go out and sleep with the other dogs? Do you think I expected something like that? It was a lightning strike! Not my fault." I take a deep breath.

Surprised at the anger in me, he says meekly, "I was depressed."

"You were depressed. Yea, well I was horrified. And I had to take care of her. Don't you think I cried and hated Mata?"

"Sunshine was the last slip in a series of slides down the tube for me." He shrugged away his guilt. "Burglary, bad weather, then bloody murder."

"Remember you gave the dog to Diego. I had to tell him the bad news. He was crushed, but didn't blame me for his loss. We were as sad to lose her as you were."

"You never said you were sorry."

"I was devastated."

"But you never said."

"It's a great image—ripping up my photo. So symbolic. Just like Mata ripping off Sunshine's head? What kind of boyfriend are you? Of course I was sorry, not just for me, but especially for you and Diego."

"Why?"

"Why?" I repeat, stung. Uneasy laughter masks my hurt. I shrug my shoulders, give him a sad little kiss on the cheek, turn and walk away.

Alligator Dreams

The summer sun reflects off the hood of the old Jeep as we bump along, following the fence line through pastureland, stands of longleaf pines, hammocks of sabal palms and old oaks. A canoe painted with blue otters and egrets is lashed to the roof. I'm feeling as young and healthy as I did in high school: sturdy body, short-cropped curly hair and tanned face devoid of makeup. In the passenger seat, my oldest friend Kate has a far-off look in her deep sky eyes. My golden retriever Mata hangs his head out the back window, ears and tongue flapping, tail wagging. He knows where we're going.

We've met up at our 40th high school reunion, and have decided to relive our past by returning to the site of some of our best times together—the Myakka River. This still unspoiled river far inland from the beaches is one of the few parts of Florida not affected by the rage of development.

"Can you believe it's been forty years," Kate sighs.

"I still feel like I'm seventeen, but thank God I don't think like I'm seventeen."

Stopping at a locked cattle-gate partially hidden by the thick south Florida undergrowth, I jump out of the Jeep to open it, avoid the puddles, climb back in and change gears. "Better use four-wheel drive. The road's under water."

"Think we ought to turn around?"

"It's not that bad. Have you lost your spunk?"

Kate laughs. "Guess it'll be another one of our adventures."

The tires spray fans of water on both sides as puddles widen into shallow ponds. We stop at a decrepit hunting cabin and get out. What's left of the road has disappeared into the swamp.

"Well, that settles it, Danielle. Let's go back to the beach."

"Oh, come on Kate. We're not going to let a little flooding stop us, are we? So what if we can't drive all the way to the river? We brought the canoe, we can put in here and find the main stream."

Mata has already jumped out of the car and heads straight for the water. Kate swallows her fear as we lift off the canoe. We grab paddles and towels, retrieve Mata, and push off. The reflected canopy quivers as the canoe cuts through the quiet water.

"I've never seen the water this high. The river's everywhere. How eerie!" The thick hammock of oaks and palms is sliced in half by the flooded river, hiding the bottom, reflecting the top. Kate takes a deep breath and exhales. "My God, I'd forgotten how beautiful it is. A steamy jungle."

A sudden splash disturbs the silence. We turn to see a turtle, the flash of its white underside somehow caught in the crook of a half-submerged tree.

"Kate, back paddle. Time to play God." I reach out over the

water, balancing myself, and flip the turtle over. The thrashing flippers churn the tea-colored water as it disappears. "How strange!"

"I've never seen a turtle hung up like that. The alligators would've had an easy treat if we hadn't drifted by."

A shock of recollection flashes across Kate's face. "I've seen this before somehow. And not just once."

I straighten the canoe, laughing, "You and your premonitions. "Can't life just happen? Don't make it out to be more than that."

"I can't help it. My visions give me some control over my life. Faith helps, too. I pray and wait for answers."

"And do they come?" A slight smile on Danielle's face.

"I get signs, feelings. I used to ignore them, but not anymore."

"Well, where do they come from?"

"Who knows?"

"I do remember when you started having those deja vu experiences in high school. They used to scare the shit out of you."

"That's when I started trusting in God."

"Whatever that is. At least you're not a missionary about it."

"No, but I can't ignore the signs. Do you remember the time I found Jeff in the woods with a broken leg?"

"I do." It was surreal. Kate had been bending over the oven when an uneasy feeling had come over her about her son. She'd shoved the feeling away, finished baking and lay down to take a nap. A vision had flashed through her mind. She'd seen him trapped under his upturned snowmobile in the deep woods. She'd immediately jumped into the car and raced toward where she thought he might be. Following her instincts, she'd found him just as she'd perceived, pulled him from the wreckage and drove him to the hospital.

"If I hadn't acted on my impulses that time, he would have frozen to death out there."

"It's true, you saved him."

We paddle in silence. Kate wonders why these old memories keep popping up. She pushes them back and concentrates on the wild beauty around her. The sun penetrates through the trees above, turning the dark water translucent.

I break the spell. "I acknowledge your beliefs. I hope you do mine."

"Let's hear them."

"Well, I just learned a new word—solipsism. It pretty much sums up my belief that the only thing someone can be sure of is that she exists."

"Not very inspirational."

"I don't want to spend precious time fearing the unknown. I believe in living in the now. I've both hated and loved my years married with kids, and my years living alone. Now I'm happy with something in between. Nothing's perfect. And nothing lasts forever."

"But you believe in dreams?"

"I believe in dreaming. A different reality. Where else could I experience my body as undulating rainbow energy particles?"

"Heh. Heh. And you think my psychic dreams are weird?"

We glide into the main current, and paddle around the bend to Rocky Ford. Old oaks draped in Spanish moss frame the clearing, shading the picnic table near the edge of the narrow white sand beach. The amber water, tinted by the tannic acid of the trees' roots, gently laps the shore.

As the canoe touches land, Mata leaps into the water, tail wagging wildly. I step ashore and tie up to a protruding root. Dropping my khaki shorts and tank top, I slip into the water after him.

Kate lingers behind, uncomfortable with the water's dark opacity, and watches my head disappear. I can see her thinking, *That's just stupid. God, how can she swim in that murky water?*

I surface. "Come on in. It's cool. You can duck under and get away from the deerflies." I bob up and down in the water, playing with Mata.

"No way I'm going in that water. I don't care how hot I am."

"Your loss."

Kate looks nervously around, then at me. "You still look great, after all these years."

"Thanks."

"It must be your lifestyle," Kate sighs. "Always rafting, hiking, or something. I stay home and eat too much."

Up the river to where it disappears around the bend, the old oak that graces the banks of Rocky Ford is submerged up to its lower branches. It looks so peaceful. I reminisce about those days long past: hanging out with Kate, sunning on the beach discussing life, swinging from the rope tied to the branch of that very oak.

Just as Kate's beginning to relax she catches a movement, a shadow, under the oak leaves. She stares, trying to focus on the spot. The ridged outline of a huge head and snout take shape.

She squints, willing it to disappear. It doesn't. She screams. "Alligator! Danielle, get out! Get out!"

I turn, irritated, "Jesus, what's gotten into y…?" and freeze. Seeing the look of terror on Kate's face I follow her gaze to a man-sized reptile just a few feet away. It begins gliding in my direction, then submerges. I make my move: swimming, flailing, leaping towards shore, expecting the clamp of jaws on my ankle, yanking me under. Kate's voice continues to shrill in the background. I reach shore hands first, then on all fours.

Then I remember the dog still in the water. Shout "Mata! Mata! Come!" Our screams frighten him, "Now!" He holds back. I lunge out over the water, grab his collar and flip his big body to shore.

Kate's sobbing uncontrollably. Her face, drained of color, accentuates the deep blue of fear in her eyes. "I couldn't save you," she cried.

"Holy shit! You did! You screamed." We cling to each other, laughing hysterically, not so brave now. Mata hangs close to my side, very quiet. Unaware of what has happened.

Suddenly Kate shudders. "Oh Danielle, the nightmare! The one the turtle reminded me of. It was a gator! Huge. With mean glinty eyes. I've had it over and over. I never knew that it was attacking you. I always woke up first."

"Well, it's over now. And I'm alive, thanks to you. You won't have that dream anymore."

The day's tranquility shattered, we prepare to leave. Paddling the canoe back through the swamp, the dog between us, we scan both shores ahead. Rounding the last bend we see the welcoming flash of the setting sun off the hood of the Jeep that will take us home.

"You're not going to swim in that river anymore, are you?"

I stare into the distance. "Mmmmm, I don't know, but I will be more careful. Maybe I'll call you first to see if you've had any nightmares." Her eyebrows lift.

Mata stands looking back, tail at point, eyes fixed on the water behind them. A large head silently surfaces. Two bulbous, slitty eyes watch our departure.

We drive slowly and silently out of the swamp. Once back onto the paved road, Kate speaks. "Thank God that's over with. I can't get that sinister snout out of my mind."

"Yea, I admit, I keep seeing the teeth, feeling the jaw clamping down on my legs. Yanking me under."

"We both need to let it go."

"Yeah, but I want to get a big shotgun, go back and kill that son of a bitch!"

"Whoa, where'd that come from?"

The intensity of this emotion shocks me, reminds me that I've had this feeling before. "After fear comes anger. Like when Mata attacked and killed the new puppy we'd gotten from Adrian. Then when he'd blamed me for it."

"You wanted to kill Adrian?"

"No, but I told him off and walked away.'

"And after?"

"Relief."

"Yes. Relief to be alive?"

"Free."

"I'll drink to both. Let's go celebrate."

Fault Lines

I've been staying away from Costa Rica, keeping busy teaching. I needed time away from Adrian after the puppy fiasco, but we are e-mailing again. It's always been the best part of our relationship—discussing politics, spirituality, philosophy. Nothing personal. Well, that and sex.

I lie in bed drifting in and out of sleep, savoring my Saturday morning laziness. My thoughts wander to our latest communication:

> "Even though we're not together all the time, I don't want to lose your loving. Where could I ever replace you? At the whore shack on the beach? A few beers, the perfume, a couple of colones? Lust could be satisfied, but would it last beyond the zip? I have a taste for you who has made no commitment but to the truth. You, with the grace of a countess, the touch of a mother, the lust of a bear. Just say Baby, I miss you so bad."

What a poet. I return:

"Neither have you made that commitment, but the truth is good. So I'm saying, Baby, I miss you so bad, and remember holding a hank of your curls in one fist, breathless, as your fingers trace a path across my skin, you crazy, beautiful, unpredictable man."

My dreams return thick and heavy in which Adrian delights me with gentle morning lovemaking and fresh ground coffee served out on the balcony overlooking the sea. I awaken and shake the dreams from my head, ready to book a trip back to Costa Rica. I get online and 'ding' I've got mail—from Adrian:

"Hi Danielle, have to make an emergency trip to Costa Rica to take care of some bank business. If you're there, don't be surprised if I sneak up behind you at the bistro on the beach and kiss your neck while you're drinking coffee."

How can two sentences make my heart pound? Damn it! That's the thing about being in love. It doesn't just stop, even in this dog-eat-dog world. The separation has been good; dulled the hurt, but not the attraction. Is it strong enough to hammer out a compromise, discover what we can and can't accept?

* * *

My arrival in Costa Rica is earth shaking. Exhausted, I sit out on the balcony in the deep dark of a rain-clouded night. The tremors begin, continue, grow into quakes, go on forever. They mimic the panic that pulsates through my body. Dear

Lord, I'm going to die! Dread hangs from my shoulders, its sharp points gouging my flesh with each quick turn of my head. I can't breathe. My heart beats pain through my chest. My legs are paralyzed.

Windows rattle, floors shake, instinct finally kicks in. Expecting the massive hardwood beams to crush me, I lower my head and run outside—to utter stillness. I'm still shaking, but nothing else is. I let out my breath in a loud whoosh and stand still as fear drains from me like grains of sand through an hourglass. I'm okay. I take one heavy-footed step after another back into the house and scan the scene.

Pictures have fallen off the walls, dishes lie broken on the floor, but the ceilings, floors and walls seem intact. I've felt tremors before but this was a fucking earthquake. Thank God my house is built to shake, rattle and roll, but not to crack and fall. I live on the fault lines of three plates of the earth's crust. What a homecoming!

I fall into bed, but the still circulating dregs of adrenalin keep my body alert and my mind possessed with thoughts of life, death, now and hereafter. I was just coming to terms with my new Theory of Everything; the quantum physics view that we are all particles of some universal energy with no beginning or end. The scientist in me affirms this connectivity much better than a divine involvement in the universe, the mess of religion. Yet when fear struck, I invoked God. Old habits? Shit. When it comes to death neither science nor religion has a definitive answer. Pondering the enigma that is life, I fall into sleep.

I awaken at sunrise to a normal looking earth, and relish the mundane pleasure of *café con leche* on the balcony. Adrian calls. "Wow, quite an entrance!"

"You sound cheerful. You loved it! You're such a disaster seeker." I chuckle. "Did you get a lot of damage?"

"Nah, falling books, paintings, but it seemed big and endless. You?"

"Just some broken glass, fallen objects, but it scared the shit out of me. I'm going to check outside next. Wanna join me? We can take a hike down to the river."

"Sure. You know I've missed you."

"Me, too." Here we go again. After ten years of ins and outs living on opposite sides of the U.S. and when we're both in Costa Rica, in separate houses, absence makes our hearts grow fonder. If this relationship is going to continue and work, we need more than absence. We've been more open with each other since communicating by e-mail, and even if it's only in writing, that's a start. Now let's see if we can do it face-to-face.

My heart pounds as I watch him walk up the muddy drive. My whole body is a smile.

"Hi Beautiful." He reaches forward, first with his lips, his arms encircling me.

He looks good, too. "Hi handsome." I hug him hard. "Best to go slow, it's so slippery…, huh, both literally and figuratively."

"Yea, Mercury's in retrograde. All kinds of eerie things are possible."

We take the trail starting on the ridge. A downed tree blocks our way. This is not unusual in a tropical area like Costa Rica: warm climate, huge rainfalls, thin topsoil, frequent earthquakes. When I try to go around, I almost fall into a newly opened rift in the earth hidden by the felled tree. "Adrian, watch out! There's a big hole. I knew the quake was long, but not this strong."

"I Googled it. 6.5. That's not small."

"The sides are steep, but it's not too deep." I throw a rock in. "Seems solid, but really slippery." My heart thumps and my head starts to tingle as I slide in. "My scalp feels like a hot iron burning from the inside out."

"What's that all about?"

"I'm not sure. An unknown allergy or a warning?"

"Maybe it's a sign."

"Hmmm. The metates." I recall the ancient corn-grinding tables we'd found while digging a new garbage pit—a meter below the surface and about a hundred feet from the ridge. "If there're artifacts, there might be graves."

"You should never have removed them."

"Science clashes with religion once again."

"Smart ass."

I poke around gingerly, "It's really too wet for digging. So hot and sticky."

With a cocky smile he offers me a hand up. "Let's get out of here."

Before turning off the ridge into the jungle, we scan the huge expanse of blue sea sliced by an even bigger sky. A cool breeze blows up over the edge of the cliff into our faces. Below a delta, like a geographic tongue cut deeply by two rivers, uncurls into a spit of land, the Whale's Tail, slapping the sea. The whipped cream surf whitens the shore on both sides. Life looks delicious with my back to the land.

"Off to the river." Hand in hand we turn into the dark humid jungle.

* * *

I have chosen to spend my life on the same mountain as the ancient indigenous people: a lookout over a vast expanse of coastline with a constant breeze blowing over it from the sea, fresh clean water rising from a spring nearby, a river flowing with life in the gorge below. The locals call it El Paraiso. I want to know more about the Diquis natives whose place I share.

In the coming week I verify that the Pre-Columbian Diquis' villages were built on ridges overlooking the sea, and their burial sites above that, sometimes surrounded by their personal effects of jade and gold pendants, stone metates and clay pottery.

My property reaches from the ridge overlooking the sea where my house is built down the opposite side to the river. The *Tico* family who homesteaded the farm over sixty years ago has shown us every inch and told us stories from the past, including finding Pre-Columbian artifacts which they've shared with us. The *patron* has pointed out this very ridge as a likely spot for a burial ground because of the many oval-shaped cobble stones covering the ground.

I need to stand back and weigh the odds here. Is this event covered in my Theory of Everything? I've never been scared off by spooky ghost stories, although during my youth I'd read the miraculous stories of the saints and believed it all, right down to the bleeding hands and feet and the real tears dripping from the statues' eyes. Now, I don't believe in souls being trapped beneath the earth, or for that matter rising up to a heaven of angels, but I try to allow other people their beliefs. Digging up dead bodies and their artifacts is a means of learning from the past, not of being haunted.

The next few days are clear and sunny enough to dry things out for a while, and give us a break from the long rainy season. My curiosity gets the best of me. I want an accomplice and call Adrian to join me. He bows out. "Uhh, I'm kind of busy today especially if it involves digging up graves."

"Oh come on. You don't really believe in ghosts?"

"Of course I do. And astrology, shamans, conspiracy theories and witches. You want to know how to neutralize a hex?"

"No. I don't believe in witches or your conspiracy theories." I cut through his effervescence, and ring off quickly, "Okay...talk later."

So, I go it alone. Junior archaeologist is my new avocation. I've studied excavating methods from the experts so I don't ruin or break any worthwhile finds. I gather some simple equipment to carry to the site: a bucket, trowel, ice pick and brush, and my camera. Digging in the fine dry clay is almost as hard as when it's wet and sucky. Fragile bones and artifacts must be carefully uncovered before attempting removal. My body relaxes into the rhythm and my mind follows. I'm caught by the thrill of the hunt, as Adrian is by the turning of his pottery wheel, or his delving into world intrigue. Things we do best alone.

After uncovering and prying out cobble after cobble, the trowel hits something decidedly metallic. The original metates and statues of their gods were made from a strange form of gray volcanic rock that almost looks and feels like concrete. I carefully scratch and dust away the clay until I see a smooth rounded granite-like surface. I continue to dig and scratch and dust, looking for an edge, but there is none. It must be huge! It looks like one of the rare perfectly round Pre-Columbian spheres only found in the Diquis Delta. Of course my scalp's tingling, my whole body is. I'm sweating like a pig from the exertion, excitement, humidity and heat, but I must finally give up as the sun drops behind the mountain. It's time for the experts to take over.

I've been in touch with an expert Costa Rican archaeologist who has verified that the metates we found were very primitive examples probably from the Diquis people, but nothing spectacular enough to warrant a professional dig. This is different! I send him a quick e-mail with photos of what I've found so far. Am I prepared to turn over my farm to the University of Costa Rica archaeology department while they dig up ancient artifacts? Do I have visions of grandeur?

That night my dreams morph into nightmares. Great rifts appear not only in the earth, but the sea and the sky, from which strange bony specters drift, surrounding the more substantial visions of Adrian and me. Nightmares mean decisions and upon arising, I make two. First, I choose science over spooks just in time to find an e-mail from the archaeologist. He's very excited. No one has found a giant Diquis sphere on this mountain before, although several have been found a few miles south. Can I pick him up at the regional airport next day for an eyewitness account? I'm a treasure seeker. I say "Yes!"

Then I call Adrian to apologize. "Hey Babe, I'm sorry I was short with you."

"Let's just forget it. I've moved on." He sounds excited, "I've found a used pottery wheel, clay included." He used to have a pottery studio and has missed practicing his craft in Costa Rica. "I can't wait to get back on the wheel."

"Splendid." I'm surprised at his quick turn around. "And

I've got great news, too." I tell him about my find and the archaeologist's coming visit. He's heard of the man, who is not only an expert on indigenous tribes, but also their clay and stone artifacts.

"I'll drive you to the airport," he offers, "I'd like to meet him too." I accept.

The next morning I jump into his car and give him a kiss. He's silent and his face has that strained, uncommunicative look. "Hi Honey. Something's wrong. What?" I ask.

"Ohhh, my neighbor just told me I was stupid."

"Why?"

"For leaving my car at the "rip-off-the-Gringo" garage and paying double."

"Well, it was your choice. It's fixed isn't it? Don't let that neighbor get you down."

"And while I'm down, I've been thinking, you don't want me to talk about my theories of witches and conspiracies? Are you censoring me?"

My throat catches. Here it comes. There are always going to be quakes on the fault line between us. Sometimes we can hold each other up through the shaking, but at others we must learn to stand alone on each side of the rift. We have found each other late in our lives, with no less passion, but more independence.

I repeat, "I'm sorry. I wanted a co-conspirator in my digging. I was wrong to get irritated by your rebuff. We both need a lot of space."

Silence.

I look at him, tears ready to spill, my heart in my mouth. I swallow and continue. "Kahlil Gibran agrees: 'Let there be spaces in our togetherness, And let the winds of the heavens dance between us'."

His steely face turns toward me and...softens. He speaks, "Then Gibran continues: 'Love each other, but make not a bond of love: Let it rather be a moving sea between the shores of our souls.' " He smiles and adds, "We've just crossed those seas to spend some time together. I'm sorry, too. What can I do to make this better?"

Stunned, I hesitate, "Uhh, can we laugh and have some fun?"

Smiling, he reaches out and covers my hand with his. "It's a deal."

We drive on in silence, physically in contact, our thoughts drifting: his to the beautiful pots he'll be throwing and mine to the treasures I'll find.

Free to Bloom   95

Jill Green, Author

Born in California, raised in Florida, retired in Costa Rica and traveling the world in between, Jill spends her time writing, teaching, volunteering, and discovering the great outdoors with her family and friends. She writes articles and stories for small magazines. This is her first book.

CPSIA information can be obtained at www.ICGtesting.com
228162LV00003B/4/P

9 780984 617722